DARK HARVEST

ELISABETH
WATHEN

DARK HARVEST

Elisabeth Wathen

CONTENTS

CONTENTS

For all the children who believe
there is something beyond our small,
beautiful planet, and who love it
enough to do what ever it takes to
protect it for the generations to come.

Cover Art Design by Amelia Wathen Engstrom, 2023

FOREWORD: 1974

"There's a hole in our galaxy."

"Vera, be serious. The data don't show—"

"Don't patronize me, Ken," her voice was low, intense. "Look."

From his hiding place under the counter, wedged between a file cabinet and a stack of drawers, twelve-year-old Ricky Menkel heard her take a few steps, then the sound of paper rustling.

"Here, see? And here. And again, here. The new radiospectography we're getting from Skylab is the best we've ever seen and shows an unmistakably erratic variation in gravity in the Alpha Aurigae system—but according to what we know about twin suns in a system like this, these variations should be impossible. If you accept Zwicky's theory on dark matter—"

"Most people still don't."

"—I know, but *we know better*, and according to him these irregularities in the gravity field of this binary system should be impossible. There's something wrong, a missing piece."

"You talk about it like it's a puzzle."

"It is," her words seemed alive, electric, they seared Ricky's brain. "Ken, this isn't a gap in our data. According to Zwicky, the halo of dark matter should be causing the gravity field to allow the expected detection of gas emission that we've observed with total consistency everywhere else we've looked.

But it's not—*look*!" Ricky heard the slap of her hand against the paper. "The only thing that makes these numbers add up is if a piece is missing from what should be there, like...a tear in the fabric of space. It's throwing everything out of balance. It's a hole that's changing the laws of physics."

The two adults were silent. Ricky's mind felt like it was on fire. He used every ounce of self-control to stay silent, hidden.

The man spoke again.

"We're already late for the meeting." Ricky heard the sound of paper being folded, a drawer opening and closing. "Let's just keep this to ourselves for now. Until we have more data."

The woman blew out a breath and laughed. When she spoke it was quiet, the tension gone.

"Ah Kenny, always the conservative voice. What would I do without you to rein me in?" The man chuckled, and Ricky heard their footsteps move toward the door. "Don't worry. I think by now I know when to stay quiet. We'll take this back to DTM with us, hammer it into something publishable."

Just then there was a knock at the door. The hinges made a small squeak as it opened, and a new voice spoke.

"Sir, ma'am, a boy has separated from the school tour and gotten lost, we're searching the building for him. Have you seen him?"

They said that they hadn't.

"Well, keep a look out. If you find him, call security. We'll escort him back."

All three left the room.

Ricky counted to ten, then crawled out from under the counter. He opened the door slowly and checked the hall before slipping out.

The first hour of his science class's tour of the Johnson Space Center had been a huge disappointment: nothing but walking down halls and peering through windows, listening to a guide wearing a blue sport coat with the NASA insignia on the lapel prattle on about why Houston was chosen to house the space center and the generosity of the President in funding it.

When they took a tram to the buildings that housed training and Control facilities his hopes had risen—maybe *there* he'd see something worthwhile—but once inside the building, there were just more hallways, more boring speeches.

Ricky's impatience got the better of him.

He worked his way to the back of the group, stopped listening to the guide, and turned on his brain.

Somewhere in this place are the labs where discoveries get made.

He was not about to pass up an opportunity to see the actual labs where scientists searched for the truths hidden among the stars.

He kept an eye on the guide, and when his head turned, Ricky ducked down a different hallway. He walked quickly, reading names on the doors, putting his eye up to narrow windows and peering inside.

Finally, he found a room that looked promising. There was no one inside. He pulled the door open and went in.

It felt like coming home.

Instruments, computational devices, video screens blinking, humming machines spooling out strips of paper with long streams of numbers on them. This was the kind of place he dreamed of working in one day. He walked around, trying to guess what each machine did, how it was used to unravel the mysteries of the cosmos.

Then he heard the door open.

He ducked into a hollow space under one of the long counters, wedging himself between some furniture, and listened. At some point he'd put his own hand over his mouth to keep from making a sound—his blood raced as he became certain that the woman was Dr. Vera Rubin, one of the foremost astrophysicists in the world.

Now, as he hurried back down the corridor toward where he'd left his tour group, he barely felt his feet touch the floor.

He knew he'd get in trouble for this.

He didn't care.

He turned a corner and was spotted by a pair of security guards. They took him to an office where he was lectured about safety and respect and setting a good example. There were threats of consequences and predictions of a dark future for a boy who doesn't behave better on school field trips. He was informed that his parents would be notified.

He didn't hear a single word.

Because Ricky was light-years away, thinking about the vast stretches of space beyond Earth, imagining the magnificent spiraling arms of the Milky Way and trying to see in his mind's eye, somewhere in the depths of the infinite universe, a jagged, gaping hole.

A'RI

The blue and red lights hovered over the machine's surface. Slowly they got closer.

Closer.

Then: purple!

A'ri swept the stylus across the space beneath the light, spun it in the closing shapes, pulled up the cryptovision image.

There she was!

Windows of safety were short. A'ri had to make the most of every second, to keep her engaged, build her trust. She was everything he'd hoped for, perfect for his purposes. His plan for making contact worked; now she liked him, trusted him. The time was coming when he would have to find a way to explain it all to her. Without frightening her. Without over-whelming her.

Without losing her.

Before beginning their weekly text conversation, for just a breath of time, A'ri allowed himself to imagine what life *could* be—if everything worked—a vision of what made it worth risking so much.

It was time to send his text.

Hi. It's me. How's it going?

QUESTIONS

Under the sheet the air was warm. Billie could feel sweat prickling on her upper lip and wiped it away. Her bedroom door was closed but being under the sheet made her feel better anyway; she wanted the extra seconds it would give her to shove her phone under the pillow if her parents came in to check on her. She wasn't supposed to be on her phone after bedtime—that was part of the deal they made when they got it for her. Normally she wouldn't break her promise to them, except this was *important.*

It started with a text message from a wrong number. Somehow she ended up having a whole conversation, and now Billie thought of this kid as a friend. She knew her parents would go nuts about it. They'd lecture her about internet stalkers, threaten to take her phone away. But she trusted her own instincts: A'ri was just a kid like her. But she was sure that her parents wouldn't listen. So she had to keep the whole thing secret.

A'ri lived far away—Billie thought maybe in Europe, possibly even in Russia or something—so they could only text at strange times, like after bedtime, when she wasn't supposed to be on her phone.

"Ugh!" she blew her breath out, fluffing her bangs away from her forehead, which was beginning to get sticky, too. "Come on!" She tapped her screen and it lit up. It was 9:15, only 15 minutes left before their window for talking would close.

The phone had been a birthday present, her parents' way of trying to make their latest move easier for her. Her mom worked for the State Department, which meant she was sent some place new every couple of years. It never bothered her that they moved. Each new place was an adventure and a chance to make new friends. But they'd stayed in the last place, California, longer than usual and moving away had been harder. Now they were in Williamsburg, Virginia. Her new school was fine. Sixth grade wasn't too bad, so far. The kids there seemed nice, but she hadn't met anyone like Janie.

Which was why texting with A'ri made such a difference.

A'ri was smart, nice, funny. Liked the same things she liked: being outside, seeing new places, adventure movies, and science fiction. And an only child, just like her.

Billie tapped the screen again. 9:27.

The phone vibrated in her hand.

Message from A'ri: Sorry I'm late! Are you there?

Hi!

Hi! Sorry it took so long. I had to do something first. This time ok?

Yeah, but if my parents come in I'll have to get off fast.

Got it. How are you?

Glad it's Friday. You?

Major homework. Huge science project.

What about?

Dark matter—or Energy? Not sure. Have

to figure it out. Know anything about it?

No. What is it?

Supposed to be invisible stuff everywhere, or something. Has to do with gravity.

Sounds like something out of a movie!

Yeah, but it's real. I have to research it. And a guy named Menkel. Scientist who discovered it or something.

At least it's science. Could be worse.

How?

Could be Social Studies.

LOL

Gotta go. Sorry. Same time, next Sunday OK?

Yup!

She frowned as she put the phone on the charging pad. Usually they talked longer, and *not* about homework. Oh well —maybe next time she'd find out what the deal was on A'ri's end of things, why it was so hard to find time to talk. Maybe she'd find out if A'ri was a boy or a girl—the name could be either.

Was it weird that she didn't even know that?

Well, she told herself, *usually you know that up front; it's kind of awkward to ask once you've started talking. And what does it matter, anyway?*

She yawned and rolled over, her sleepy mind wondering what that dark matter stuff was all about. If it's supposed to be everywhere, she hoped that it was a good thing.

CHAPTER

3

A NEW FRIEND

"I promise we won't stay too long. I've only got two students to meet with, 45 minutes each." Billie's dad was driving them to the library on a Saturday. He tutored high school students in math on weekends.

"It's fine," Billie was looking out the window, taking in the town she was just starting to get to know. "I like libraries. And I have stuff to do, too."

It only took ten minutes to drive to the library, which was just past the old colonial center of town. Billie was still amazed at seeing people walk down the street dressed up as if it was 300 years ago, men looking like George Washington, and women wearing white caps, long dresses and aprons. She'd seen them at bus stops and in grocery stores, just like anyone. She knew it meant they worked in the colonial village, but she still wasn't used to it. When they walked into the library they passed one of them. She couldn't help staring.

"How about if we go visit the colonial stuff tomorrow?" Her father whispered in her ear. "Since we live here, we can do everything for free. We could take some tours...?"

Billie knew he was trying to do things to help her to feel at home in their new town. Mom being out of town for work made him try even harder. She wanted to tell him to relax, she was fine, but she also wanted to see some of the colonial stuff, so she nodded and said, "Sure, that'd be cool."

"Great. I'm meeting my first student over there," he pointed across the room to a wide, open area with lots of tables. "See you back here in two hours?"

"Sure," Billie said. "See ya later."

He smiled at her and headed off.

Billie looked around. She didn't have any homework to do, so she decided to kill some time online before heading to the juvenile books section. At the far end of the room stood a bank of computers, each in its own little desk area, with a sign that said, "30 Minutes Per Person—sign in at Reference Desk." She found the reference desk and walked over to ask where she could sign up for a computer.

"For catalogue purposes, or internet?" a short woman with a soft voice and thick glasses asked.

"Um, internet I guess."

"Put your name here," the librarian pushed a clip board toward her and pointed to a line. When Billie had written her name down, the librarian wrote the number 4 next to it, and pointed out which computer was hers.

Billie logged in. With nothing particular in mind, she decided to go to Google Earth and check things out from space. Thinking about space reminded her of the conversation with A'ri, and she decided to find out more. She quickly checked her texts, then typed "Menkel scientist, dark matter" in the search window.

A page full of links to websites and science publications blinked onto the screen in front of her. A lot of it looked like it was written in a different language, so she picked the easiest to begin with—Wikipedia. The page on dark matter was hard to understand, so she clicked back to one on Menkel.

A Dr. Richard Menkel turned out to be a scientist who had done a lot of work on dark matter, but what that was she wasn't sure—the scientific stuff was really dense. The part about his life was pretty interesting, though. She discovered that he'd moved around a lot as a kid, graduated early, and went to college when he was only 15. She said, "Wow!" a little too loudly and got shushed when she read that he was currently a professor at Stanford University in Palo Alto, California. Their house had only been half a mile from Stanford. She wondered if she'd ever passed him on the street.

It turned out that one of the things he was most famous for was a book about dark matter that was supposed to make the concept easy for anyone to understand.

"That sounds good," Billie muttered. She wrote down the title on a little piece of scratch paper. Then she logged out and went back to the reference desk. Handing the paper to the librarian she asked, "Can you tell me if the library has this book?"

"It's currently checked out, and there's a waiting list," she answered after a few keystrokes. "Would you like to be added to the list? We can notify you by email or text when the volume is available for you to check out."

Billie said yes, but nothing could be done until she had a library card. For that, she had to go to the front desk. Ten minutes later Billie had a brand-new library card and had been placed on the waiting list.

She still had some time before Dad would be ready to go. Billie decided to go see if she could find something fun to read. She was walking slowing along the shelves in the Sci-Fi section, letting her finger trail along the edges of the books as she read their titles, when she felt a tap on her shoulder.

"Excuse me, did I hear you asking to be put on the waiting list for the Menkel book about dark matter?"

Billie turned around. She was looking at a boy who was about her height, wore glasses, and had straight black hair. He looked like he was probably about her age.

"Uh, yeah, I did," she said.

"Me too!" he exclaimed, and Billie saw the lady behind the juvenile desk glare in their direction. "That's so cool! Not many people know about Dr. Menkel or have even heard of dark matter!"

He was clearly from the nerdy side of the tracks, but he seemed nice. She nodded and started walking toward a far corner of the room, away from the disapproving librarian.

"A friend of mine told me about him," she said in a hushed voice. "I also just found out that he lives in California, the same town I just moved from—"

"No way!" the boy said, again too loudly. This time Billie put a finger to her lips and jerked her head in the direction of the Youth Desk. "Oops, yeah, sorry," he shrugged. "But that's so cool! You lived in Palo Alto? Did you ever visit Stanford University?"

Billie lowered herself to the carpet and put her books on the floor. The boy joined her, crossing his legs and leaning forward eagerly. "We lived pretty close to it, actually. Sometimes we'd take hikes in the hills behind Stanford, and it was one of my favorite places to ride bikes with my dad. It's really pretty."

The boy squeezed his fists closed and his eyes shut and seemed to hold his breath for a minute, before exhaling and saying, "It is *totally* my dream to go there one day. I just hope Dr. Menkel is still there by the time I get to college—he's *completely* my *maximum* hero in the whole world!"

"Well, I don't know much about Menkel, but I can tell you a lot about Stanford. And hey," she held out a hand, "my name is Billie."

"Oh my gosh," he grabbed her hand and started shaking it, words galloping out of his mouth. "Of course! My name is Reuben, Reuben Murray, I'm 12 and I go to Hamilton Middle School, 7th grade, and it's really nice to meet you, too!"

"Hamilton?" Billie said. "Me too! But I'm in 6th."

"That's great! It's the best middle school in the 'Burg. Who're your teachers?"

They compared class schedules and discovered that they had the same lunch period, and their lockers were close by each other.

Suddenly Billie remembered the time.

"Reuben, I have to go—my dad is waiting for me upstairs," she stood quickly.

Reuben jumped up too. "Come find me at lunch—I'll introduce you to my friends. We're a motley crew, but we have a lot of fun."

Billie giggled. *Motley crew?* "Sure, sounds good. I'll look for you Monday. See you!"

"Great meeting you!" Reuben called after her, loudly enough that the juvenile desk lady stood up and glared at him.

A MOTLEY CREW

"Billie! Over here!"

She looked around the crowded cafeteria. Reuben was waving at her from a table up against the far wall. Billie made her way over with her lunch tray and sat in a free space across from him.

"Hi," she said, and smiled.

"You found us!" Reuben grinned. "Guys, this is Billie. Billie, this is Thomas, Ben, Gaurav, Nira and Shae." Billy looked around at the faces of the kids sitting with him. She had no idea which names belonged to which.

"Jeeze Ru," one of the girls said, rolling her eyes. "How's she gonna know who's who?" She looked at Billie and pointed to herself. "I'm Nira. I'm in 6th grade, and I think I recognize you from English, right?" Billie nodded. Nira had long, black hair and huge brown eyes. "That is my brother Gaurav," she pointed across the table to a boy with lots of messy curls that needed cutting. "He's in 8th grade and thinks he knows everything." She stuck her tongue out at him, and he laughed.

"True. Also, I'm the pretty one," Gaurav said, then yelped because Nira kicked him under the table.

"This is Shae," Nira continued, pointing to a pale, redheaded girl with lots of freckles on Billie's left. "She's in 7th grade. Thomas, also in our grade, is next to her, and Ben is the guy who keeps us safe." Ben was huge, like a football player, easily six feet tall and refrigerator-sized. He smiled shyly at Billie, his teeth brilliant white against his dark skin.

"I only look dangerous, but we don't get messed with too much, even though—"

"We definitely move in our own orbit!" Reuben finished, throwing his head back dramatically.

Everyone else groaned. Shae leaned toward Billie and pretended to whisper, "We let him say that stuff, it's just his way. He's so *dramatique*!" Some of the others chuckled, including Reuben.

"Someone's got to light a fire under you guys," he said, reaching into a brown bag and pulling out a sandwich. "If I didn't overdo it sometimes, you'd all just sit around like bumps on a log, nothing would ever get done."

"Uh, so, you guys *do* things? Are you a club or something?" Billie asked.

"Not really," Thomas spoke up. He was shorter than the other boys, his hair a sandy brown, his face sunburned. "I mean, homework sometimes, but mostly we just hang out." He grinned across the table at her and bit into a large apple.

"We're definitely the most interesting people in the whole school," Nira said with a smirk. "Nobody else is really worth wasting your time with."

Billie put a forkful of chili in her mouth because she wasn't sure how to answer. She liked them, they seemed nice and kind of funny. But she tried to avoid cliques and kids who exclude others.

"It's not like that," Shae said to her, quietly.

"Like what?" Billie asked, confused.

"What you're thinking, we're not like that," Shae explained, "not exclusive. It's more like…"

"The truth is that *we're* the ones who get excluded," Gaurav said, wiping his mouth with the back of his hand. "We're the kids no one else wants to be friends with, so…" he shrugged.

"We found each other, and stick together," Reuben finished. "Anybody's welcome to join us, but no one really wants to," he shrugged. "Instead of miserable loners, we revel in each other's fellowship."

Ben made an impatient sound. "Don't talk like an encyclopedia, Ru, you sound pretentious."

"He *is* pretentious," Nira said.

"A pretentious wannabe physicist drama queen," Thomas laughed.

The bell rang. Lunch was over.

Billie had PE after lunch. As she walked to the locker room, she couldn't help smiling. She'd never met a group of kids like that, they were different for sure—but she *did* like them. They were comfortable just being themselves, unlike so many other kids who always seemed to be posing, faking it, worried about what everyone else thought. She liked the way they teased Reuben, but in a way that showed that they liked him, not mean at all.

Kind of like family.

The next day in English, Nira pushed out the chair in the desk next to hers. "Come sit by me," she smiled at Billie. When she'd pulled her things out of her backpack, Nira asked, "So how do you like Hamilton?"

"It's fine," Billie shrugged. "The teachers seem nice, so far at least."

"Oh yes, I think we're the best middle school," Nira agreed, "but it must be a little hard coming in from outside—most of the kids here have known each other since kindergarten."

"I'm used to moving around," Billie told her. "There's always an adjustment."

The lesson that day was about a poem by Shakespeare, and their teacher said it was all right for the students to team up to do the work. They worked together, chatting easily, until it was time to pack up. "You know," she said as she was cramming a very large binder into her over-stuffed backpack, "We get together most weekends to do homework."

"Yeah?"

"Mmm-hmm," Nira was having trouble. Billie reached over to try to help open the backpack wider, and make it easier to push the binder in. Finally, it slid down. "Thanks. Why don't you come, too?"

"Thanks," Billie said. "I mean, I'd have to ask my parents, but I'd like to."

"Great," Nira hoisted the backpack strap over one shoulder and stood just as the bell rang. "We'll be at our house, Gaurav's and mine. Give me your phone number and I can text you the address."

"So I met some kids at school," Billie said around a mouthful of mashed potatoes at dinner that night.

Her mother looked up. "Nice! Tell us about them."

"They're kinda weird, but in a good way," Billie said, and one by one described each of her new friends. "Reuben calls them the 'Motley Crew,' but I don't think that's official or anything."

"They sound like an interesting bunch," Dad said.

"They get together most weekends to do homework and stuff, and they invited me to come this weekend."

"And stuff?" Mom asked, raising an eyebrow.

Billie rolled her eyes. "You know, nothing bad...I mean they don't seem like *those* kinds of kids...just homework and hanging out. It's at Nira's house."

Her parents exchanged a look, then her father said, "I'm sure it's fine, honey, but I'm going to need Nira's parents' number, so I can just call and..."

"...check it out," Mom finished the sentence for him. They did that a lot. Mostly Billie thought it was cute, but in this case it was annoying.

"Don't you guys trust me? My instincts? I think they've proven pretty good so far," she scowled at them.

"Sweetie, you do have good instincts, and we do trust them," Mom said, "but we're new here, and it pays to be careful, that's all." She reached across the table and patted her arm. "It's not you we worry about, you know."

Billie couldn't stay mad. "I know," she puffed out a breath and half-smiled. "It's the big, bad world."

"Bingo," Dad grinned, and forked up another bite of salad.

Billie texted Nira to ask for her parents' phone number, and by the time she was ready to go to bed Dad had called and worked everything out.

"It turns out that Nira's father is someone your mother has worked with," he told her, hugging her good night.

"Yes!" her mother laughed. "Imagine my surprise when I heard the name of one of my office mates from when we were in Poland!"

"I guess that means they check out, then?" Billie tried to sound sarcastic, hoping her parents would feel silly for having worried.

"Yes ma'am," Mom said.

Something suddenly occurred to Billie. "But wait, if you worked with her dad in Poland, how come I don't remember going to school with Nira and Guarav?"

"Their father was there on his own, while the family stayed here," Dad explained. Billie knew that some families made that choice, especially once the children got a little older. Not everyone liked moving all the time; some picked a place to set-tle while the moms or dads went off on foreign assignments, visiting every few months. She was glad her parents had never decided to go that route.

Now there was another layer to her interest in her new friends, and she was looking forward to seeing them outside of school this weekend.

REUBEN'S OBSESSION

"Molly Engle, look at you!" A very tall, slim man with dark brown skin and the biggest smile Billie had ever seen held his arms out to welcome them. His words sounded faintly foreign, overly precise. "Come in, come in!"

Billie's mom, who had come to the door with her, beamed back at him. "It's been too long, Daksh."

They crossed the threshold and he wrapped her in a hug. "It has been too long, indeed," he turned from her to Billie, "which I can see by how much this young lady has grown up! The last time I saw you, you were barely walking." He reached out and put a hand on her shoulder. Billie looked at Mom with questioning eyes. She didn't remember ever meeting him before. Thankfully, Nira saved her.

"Dad, why do you always have to hug everyone?" She was hurrying over to them, frowning. "Other people's dads don't do that...don't be so..."

He threw his head back and laughed, then winked at Billie. "I embarrass my daughter all the time, and she is always quick to let me know it," he said, mostly to Mom.

"It is good to see you, Daksh. I think it's been, let me see, nearly ten years?"

"Goodness yes," Nira's father shook his head. "Too long. Won't you come in for a moment? I'd like to introduce you to Madhu after all this time," he steered her through a door, away from the girls.

"Thank goodness," Nira sighed. "He gets all emotional when he sees old friends. Ma says it's because they were so important all the time he was away from us, but I think it's just *him*." She smiled sideways at Billie. "Come on, before he wants to start telling long stories. Everyone is downstairs."

She led Billie down a hallway, through a door and down a flight of concrete stairs. The air felt cool, and they could hear music playing. At the bottom of the stairs they turned left. At the end of a short hall a huge room expanded before them.

"Billie's here," she announced. From around the room, all Reuben's friends looked up from what they were doing. "Wow!" Billie said in surprise. "This is cool!"

The basement room was enormous. The walls looked like they had been painted by kindergarteners: crude and colorful flowers, suns, green grass, fanciful creatures with wings and claws and lots of eyes, some with more than one head, as well as bunnies, birds, horses, and in a couple of places, shapes that looked like a house or castle.

"It's exactly what you think it is," Gaurav said as she stood there staring. "When we moved in, Nira and I were 4 and 6. Ma needed something to keep us busy, and since this was going to be our playroom, she just let us paint whatever we wanted."

"It took us a couple of years," Nira added, flopping down on a beanbag chair nearby. "By the time we were old enough to want to paint over it and do something different, Ma said no, it was art from our childhood, precious memories, blah blah blah," she rolled her eyes. Billie noticed she did that a lot.

"I like it," Billie said.

There were several bookshelves filled with books, a couple of large tables and desks, several beanbag chairs, and something was playing music on a small table across the room. Thomas, who was sitting at the large, central table with several books open in front of him, saw where she was looking.

"That's a record player," he said.

"A—?"

"Ma and Dad said we could have this space for our own, but no technology," Gaurav explained. "No TV's, no game systems or computers...we're not even supposed to bring our phones down here."

"But," Thomas stood up and went over to the music table, "they let them have this old thing, and all their old records, and we found a bunch more at a thrift store."

"So we can listen to music," Reuben put in, shrugging. "It's old fashioned, but..."

"It works," Thomas said, lifting a thin metal arm off the spinning vinyl disk, stopping the music, then setting it down again with a slight screech to start it again.

Billie nodded. "I get it," she said. "My parents only got me a phone this summer. Before that it was like living on a different planet from most other kids." She walked over to the large table where Thomas had been working, put down her backpack and sat down.

Thomas returned to his seat. "Nira and I were just about to get started on the poetry project for English."

"Great!"

Everyone had brought work to do—Thomas, Nira, and Billie worked on their poetry project; Gaurav and Shae were reviewing for a science test; Ben was reading, and Reuben was working on a math assignment. They worked for about two hours. Thomas changed the record several times, but the music was always quiet, and Billie liked it: it reminded her of the stuff her mother played on Sunday mornings at home.

At one point Nira and Gaurav's mother came downstairs with a tray of food and reminded them that they had piano lessons at 4:30.

"Ugh," Nira moaned when her mother was gone again. "I forgot that we had make-up lessons today." She frowned unhappily at her brother.

"You both play piano?" Billie asked.

"Yup. Same teacher since we were 5 and 7," Gaurav said.

"I hate it," Nira said, stuffing a peanut butter cracker into her mouth.

"You just don't like to practice," her brother said.

"Neither do you!"

"Yeah, but I love to play," he grinned, twiddling the fingers of both hands on an imaginary keyboard in front of him.

Nira did her eye roll thing again. "Gaurav is the musical one. He can play anything you want, just out of his head. It's amazing," she sounded sincerely proud of him.

"Yeah, but don't make me read sheet music," Gaurav shuddered dramatically, curling his fingers into fists.

Nira laughed. "He is the bane of our teacher's existence. She can't deny he has talent, but she won't let him play the way he wants."

Suddenly Reuben jumped in his chair. "Sheet music—books--that reminds me! I have something for you, Billie." He reached down into his backpack, rummaged around, and came out with a book. "It's the Menkel book. It was my turn on the waiting list, but here," he passed it across to her, "you can have it first."

"Thanks," Billie said, taking the book. "But I don't want you to lose your turn, I can wait."

Ben, who'd been quietly reading in one of the beanbag chairs closest to the record player, snorted loudly. "He's already read it. Twice. You should just take it."

Billie's eyebrows rose. "Twice?"

Reuben shrugged, grinning.

"We all know way too much about him," Shae added, looking up from the science homework she and Gaurav had been working on. "It'll be great for Ru to have someone new to gush to."

"Have you all read the book, too?"

"Might as well have," Ben answered, stretching his long legs out and yawning.

"The thing is," Thomas said, reaching for a cracker, "we're not in love with the good doctor like Ru is, but the science *is* fascinating."

"You mean dark matter?"

"Mmm-hmm," Thomas munched. "Did you know that it's everywhere?"

"Passing through everything, all of us, all the time?" Ben said, joining them at the table and reaching for some food.

"No," Billie said. "I still don't really know much about it. Sounds totally made up. Science Fiction-y."

"Right?" Nira said.

"But it's not!" Reuben exclaimed. "And Dr. Menkel is finding out more and more about it. He thinks it's more important than anyone realizes!"

"Important how?" Billie asked. "I mean, if we can't see it, and never even knew it existed for a long time, how important can it really be?"

"That's easy," Thomas said. "Just think about germs: we didn't know they existed two hundred years ago, and still can't see them without special tools. But they're hugely important, and everyone knows about them now."

"Right! That's good!" Reuben jumped up from his chair and started pacing. "He hasn't said so in any publications, but reading between the lines, I think that Dr. Menkel believes—"

"No, stop," Nira held her hand up. "None of those crazy theories of yours today, Ru. Let her read the book first. Besides," she flipped her English book closed and started piling her papers on top, "it's almost piano time, we have to clean up."

They all packed their backpacks and went upstairs together, Billie carrying the empty snack tray. They found the parents, her mother still there, sitting outside on a deck shaded by trees.

"Time to go," her mom said, standing up and smiling. "This has been so delightful. Robert and I will have you over soon, so we can all catch up."

The adults hugged, and then everyone went to the front door.

"Mom, before we go, these are my friends," Billie introduced each of the others to her mother.

"So nice to meet you all." She smiled.

On the drive home, Mom was humming happily to herself.

"I didn't know you were such good friends with them," Billie said.

"It's not that we were," Mom said, "but we did work out of the same office for two years, and worked together on some...projects. When you see someone after so long, it feels a little like coming home, know what I mean?" She looked over at Billie. "I guess when we move around so much, people are more 'home' than places. Finding one of them...it just feels nice."

"Did Dad know him, too?"

"Of course! We all got together pretty regularly."

Billie thought about this, wondering what her parents had been like back then.

Mom patted her knee. "Your friends seem like a nice group. Eclectic."

"What does that mean?"

"Um, different from each other, an interesting mix."

"Yeah," Billie laughed, "that's for sure. Especially Reuben."

"Reuben," Mom wrinkled her eyebrows, "he was the skinny one with glasses and black hair?"

"Yep," Billie reached into her backpack and pulled out the book he'd given her. "He brought me this. It's a book I need for...science...and he got it from the library first, so he let me have it."

"What's it about?"

"It's by a guy named Dr. Menkel. He explains something called dark matter—"

"Menkel?" Mom sounded funny, almost angry. "Richard Menkel?"

"I think so," Billie looked at her mother. "Why?"

"Nothing," she said, looking at the book in Billie's lap and frowning. "Just a funny coincidence, is all." She looked over at Billie. "I knew a man, a scientist, someone I worked with back in California…that's all."

Billie could read her mom pretty well. Sometimes when she talked, she used a voice that meant, "don't ask me any more questions about this." She was using that voice now.

Did her mom know Reuben's Dr. Menkel? If so, why wouldn't she want to tell Billie about it?

She turned to stare out the window for the rest of the drive home. She was going to start reading that book the *minute* they got home.

A'RI

A'RI

Hi! How are you?

Good here. You?

Fine.

Guess what: I got a book by that scientist guy, and started reading it.

The whole book?!

Not yet—but it's pretty in-teresting. Makes that dark stuff sound super important. Crazy that we still don't know much about it.

IKR! I learned a lot from that project.

Can I ask you something?

Sure

I don't mean to be weird, but are you a boy or a girl?

LOL. Boy.

Are you a kid, like me?

I'm 11.

Me too! Where do you live?

Hey—I gotta go! Same time next week?

Sure.

See you then!

A'ri's head was buzzing—he felt a little dizzy...but in a good way. *He'd told her he was a boy.* It was the first time he'd dared to do anything like that, and it felt *amazing*. Even though he'd have to keep hiding it here...the fact that Billie knew was *something*. In her mind, her world, he wasn't a blank slate, forced to fit into a mold that served the Gen, the Owners, and The

Realm. To Billie, he had an identity: he was *A'ri the boy*. That made it feel real. It made him more sure than ever about how important his mission was.

He needed to focus now. A'ri sat back in his chair and blew out a long, slow breath.

He'd expected her to ask questions at some point. She needed to know more about him to feel safe. Her sense of safety, of trust, was essential for his plan, but he couldn't let it go any further yet. She wasn't ready—and he couldn't risk losing her. Too much was at stake.

He checked to be sure there were no telltale tracks left by his transmission. When he was sure everything was clean, he shut down the interface device and closed his work space, thinking about Billie and what his next steps should be.

He was thrilled she'd taken an interest and followed up on his hints about Menkel. It was essential that she understand things on her own before he revealed everything. He thought of the Earther's story about children lost in a forest, leaving a trail of breadcrumbs to mark their path. He hoped his breadcrumbs would lead Billie to the right place—everything depended on it.

SETTLING IN

"Billie?" Her dad knocked on her door, pushing it open as he stepped into the room. He was carrying a laundry basket full of clothes. "Your laundry is done. Want help folding?"

Billie had been sitting in her window seat, staring out at the world, lost in thought. Picking up the book she'd just finished reading, she put it on her night table and walked over to her bed. "Sure Dad, thanks."

"Whatchya doing?"

"Thinking. Reading."

"Homework? Stuff for school?"

"Kinda," Billie reached into the basket and pulled out a pair of shorts. "If you're checking on me, I finished all my homework for today."

Dad chuckled, handing her a folded t-shirt. "No, sweetie, I know you get your work done. So what are you reading, then?"

"Oh, it's that book Reuben loaned me," she reached in and grabbed another shirt. "It's kind of...amazing."

"Oh?"

"Yeah, I mean, did you know that dark matter is literally everywhere?"

"I think I read about that somewhere..." Dad handed her one end of a bed sheet. "Help me with this one," he said, stepping back.

"And no one really knows why, or what it does," Billie kept talking as they matched the corners up and folded it the long way. "Seems like something so..."

"Ubiquitous?"

"Uh, if that means 'it's everywhere,' yeah," Billie handed Dad her end for the final folds. "Something so *ubiquitous* must be pretty important, but we don't even understand how."

"You and your friends read books about this stuff," Dad cocked an eyebrow at her, "for fun?"

"Not really," Billie admitted, grabbing another pair of pants from the basket. "It's actually Reuben's thing, but he talks about it a lot. Oh," she looked up, suddenly remembering something. "And I think Mom might know the guy who wrote this book. Do you know? Dr. Richard Menkel?"

Dad shook his head as he reached into the bottom of the basket for the final pair of socks. "Doesn't ring a bell. Why?"

Billie shrugged. "He works at Stanford, so he must live in Palo Alto, and Mom acted like maybe she knew who he was..."

Dad picked up the empty basket and moved it over to the corner of the room. "Ready for a refill!" he said. "She meets a lot of people in her job. Maybe that's it? Some official thing she had to attend when we were there?"

"I guess," Billie sighed. "Thanks for helping me fold."

"No problem. Dinner in an hour."

Thunderstorms and heavy rains dominated the weather, but on Friday the sun came out. At lunch, Shae suggested they take advantage of it.

"Let's go to CW after school, you guys."

"What's CW?" Billie asked.

"Sorry," Shae explained, "that's what we call the colonial part of town."

"Colonial Williamsburg, see?" Ben added.

"Oh," Billie nodded. "Do we need tickets to get in?"

"Nope!" Reuben was licking peanut butter off his fingers. "It's open to everyone."

"If we wanted to take tours we'd have to get passes," Shae said, "but I'm just talking about hanging out—there's a field next to the old courthouse we like to go to."

"No good," Gaurav spoke up. "Joey told me fife and drum is practicing there this afternoon."

"Well, we could still sit by the old oak," Ben pointed out.

"Or the witch tree!" Thomas grinned.

"It sounds to me," Nira said, leaning over the table, "as if you haven't been there yet."

"Nope," Billie said. "Dad and I were planning on going some time, but he's been busy, so we haven't done it yet."

"Perfect!" Nira nodded and looked around at the others. "Let's give her a tour!"

By the end of the school day parents had been enlisted to drive them and drop them off, and at 3:30 they were standing together in a bricked plaza at one end of a long, straight road that was closed to traffic.

"This is Merchant's Square," Reuben said, spreading his arms wide and turning in a circle. "It's not authentic colonial stuff, it's for tourists." Billie looked around at the shops and restaurants lining either side of the square. "Down there is the colonial stuff," he said, pointing.

Nira started walking. "George Washington, Thomas Jefferson, all those guys were here a lot," she said airily, waving her hand in the air.

Billie looked at the buildings lining the street as they walked, all of them simple, gabled houses with signs indicating what was inside: tailors, shoemakers, grocers, a post office, and inns. There were lots of tourist groups all wearing the same-colored t-shirts with laminated passes hanging around their necks, as well as actors dressed in colonial costumes, and horse-drawn carriages going up and down the street.

"Watch out for the horse-apples," Ben cautioned.

"Horse apples?" Billie asked, confused. Ben pointed to a steaming brown pile in the middle of the road, and she laughed, stepping carefully around it. "This is pretty cool," Billie said. "If there weren't tourists, I could almost believe that we were really back in colonial times."

"You should take some of the tours," Reuben said, nodding.

"Yeah," Shae agreed. "You can learn a lot about life back then. The interpreters really take their roles seriously. They'll talk to you as if they stepped right out of history."

"*My* favorite tours are the Lantern Tours," Thomas said.

"You and your ghost stories!" Nira rolled her eyes.

"What? They're awesome!" Thomas shot back. He turned to Billie. "See, you meet after dark, and a guide with a lantern leads you through the streets and tells you ghost stories about the different buildings."

Billie nodded. "I bet there are lots of ghosts here."

"So many!" Thomas nodded. "There are tons of books about how haunted it is, and mediums and ghost hunters come here all the time to do research."

"It's nonsense," Nira scoffed.

They led her up one street and down another, telling her about the buildings and leading her to where an ancient oak spread enormous, looping branches wider and taller than a house. They settled onto a sunny patch of grass nearby.

Billie leaned back and closed her eyes, enjoying the feel of sunlight on her face. "I like it here."

"I'm glad you've come," Nira said, stretching out on the grass beside her.

"Dad sure was happy to see your mom again," Gaurav added.

"How do your parents know each other?" Ben asked. "You've never lived here before, have you?"

"No," Billie shook her head. "Mom and Mr. Patel worked together in Europe."

"Seems like they were pretty good friends," Shae observed.

"I guess," Billie said. "I was only about two then, so I don't remember. Dad says they hung out a lot."

"Ma was here with us," Gaurav said.

"Did you like moving around all the time?" Nira propped herself up on an elbow to look at Billie.

"Mmm-hmm," Billie smiled, feeling a little sleepy from the warmth of the late afternoon sun. "It always seemed like an adventure." She paused before adding, "It was harder coming here, though, leaving my best friend in Palo Alto."

"That's right!" Reuben exclaimed. "You lived near Stanford —so lucky!"

"It's a pretty campus, but no prettier than here—CW."

Ben laughed. "He means, you're lucky to have lived close to his *hero*."

"Oh," Billie sat up and reached for her backpack. "That reminds me, here's your book back, Reuben; I finished it."

"What's the matter? Didn't you like it?" Reuben saw she was frowning as she handed it to him.

"No," Billie said. "I thought it was really interesting. But," she hesitated, then went on, "it's my mom. When she saw the book, and I told her about Dr. Menkel, she acted.... weird."

They were all looking at her now.

"Weird how?" Nira asked.

Billie shook her head. "I don't know. I just felt like...it seemed like maybe she knew him, but didn't want to talk about it, didn't want me to know that she knew him." She looked at her friends. "It was just...weird."

Gaurav nodded slowly. "Sometimes Dad gets like that." He exchanged a look with Nira, who shook her head. Ben saw them and made an impatient noise.

"Guys, just because you don't live on a military base doesn't mean we don't understand what it means that your dad works for *the government*," he put air quotes around the last two words.

Thomas snorted. "It's pretty much the worst-kept secret in town."

Billie was confused. "What? What secret?"

Reuben stood up and threw his hands out. "Never mind, just ignore them. What I want to know is: did your mom actually know Dr. Menkel?" the look of excited hope on his face made Billie smile.

"I kinda think she did, but I don't know why," Billie said, standing up herself, brushing grass off her palms, "and I don't know why she wouldn't want to talk about it." She grinned at Reuben. "I'm going to work on her, though, see what I can find out."

"You would make Ru's whole year if you could connect him," Nira laughed. "Come on, it's almost 5:00, we need to get back to the parking lot."

As they walked, Reuben fell into step beside Billie. "If you liked the book, there's more stuff he's written recently. About dark matter—he's got some interesting theories about the importance of it in the cosmic balance."

"Cool," Billie said. "Sure, I'd read more of his stuff. I mean, maybe not another whole book…"

"No, no, just an article—I'll make you a copy, okay?"

"Okay," Billie said. Normally she liked reading science *fiction*, not real science. But something seemed important about this, and Mom's reaction to Dr. Menkel's book made her think that the more she knew, the better.

QUESTIONS

The smell of something good drew Billie to the kitchen, where Dad was getting dinner ready.

"Mmm, what're you making?" she asked, lifting the lid on a pot on the stove.

"Pantry Surprise," he laughed and handed her a wooden spoon. "Stir that for me, would you?"

Billie stirred. It was thick and smelled delicious. "Lentils? Meatballs?"

"Yes to both," he said. "And in about 10 minutes you can add fresh baked flatbread to the menu."

Billie stirred quietly, thinking. "Flatbread was something slaves invented, right??"

"I'm not sure about that," her dad said. "My brain is telling me that it was invented in ancient Egypt, and they had slaves. But it also seems like the kind of thing that a lot of different cultures have their own version of." He looked over at Billie. "Why?"

"I don't know," Billie shrugged. "We're learning about slavery in Social Studies."

"American slaves? I don't think they invented flatbread."

"Guess not," Billie put the wooden spoon down and covered the pot. "We're going to a slavery museum in Richmond this week, on a field trip," Billie said. "I think it's kind of like the South's version of a holocaust museum."

"The horrors of man's inhumanity to man need to be studied and remembered by everyone," he said. "It's pretty heavy stuff. Do you want me to come on the field trip—like as a parent helper or something?"

Billie smiled. "No, it's okay."

"What's okay?" Mom came into the kitchen, sniffing appreciatively. "That smells divine. When's dinner?"

"As soon as the table's set," Dad opened the oven door and pull out several small, puffy loaves of bread. "Everything's ready."

Billie and her mother set the table, and they sat down to eat.

"What were you guys talking about when I came in?" Mom asked.

"Billie's class is going on a field trip to Richmond Thursday," Dad explained.

"Museum," Billie elaborated. "Slavery."

"Ah," Mom nodded, taking another bite. "Since Richmond was once the capitol of the Confederacy, that ought to be pretty interesting," she looked at her husband. "Remember that documentary we watched…"

Billie sat back and let her parents' conversation wash over her, paying little attention to what they were saying. Her own thoughts kept returning to her last conversation with A'ri. Something had seemed wrong, but she just couldn't put her finger on it. He'd been explaining why he had to be so careful about when he contacted her, why he was so limited, and it just didn't sound...normal.

She puzzled over it as she helped clean up after dinner was over.

He hadn't mentioned parents or strict rules or bedtimes. He didn't talk about battery life or Wi-Fi availability.

What he told her made it sound like he had almost no freedom in how he got to spend his time, no real privacy at all, and he wasn't supposed to even have friends. With the stuff they were learning in Social Studies and the field trip coming up this week, even though it sounded a little crazy Billie couldn't stop thinking that it sounded like he was more a slave than just another kid with a phone.

A slave. Was that even possible? Did slaves even still exist? Could kids be slaves?

It took three school buses to drive the entire 6th grade class to Richmond. After an hour-long presentation that included a short movie about the lives of slaves, the students were allowed to explore the museum on their own. Thomas found Nira and Billie, and the three of them stayed together. They decided to begin at the second floor "Forced Emigration" exhibit.

"This reminds me a lot of the Holocaust Museum in D.C.," Thomas said. They were standing in front of a recreation of a slave ship, with 150 people crammed into a tiny hold, chained in the dark together. "The pictures of the barracks in the concentration camps...the misery."

"Misery is right," Nira said.

They walked on to the next room.

"I used to think this was history," Thomas shook his head, "but it really isn't, is it?"

"What makes you say that?" Billie asked.

"Isn't it obvious?" Nira snapped. She walked over to a framed drawing of a group of Africans chained together at the ankles, waiting beside a platform where a white man was shouting at a crowd, auctioning them off. "It's still here. People of color make up a disproportionately large percentage of the poor, and the people in jail. They are victimized by the legal system, the education system, the healthcare system. They are not equally represented in the government. What would you call that?"

Thomas looked at Billie. "Nira won an essay contest last year, all about civil rights. She got an award for it at a special ceremony, with the Governor and everything. It's kind of her *thing* now."

"It's not just *my* thing," Nira folded her arms defiantly. "You wrote an essay, too, Thomas."

"I know, but you're the one who ended up on the news," he grinned at Billie and shrugged.

"But...do you think slavery is still happening?" Billie said. "I don't mean just racism, but people actually owning other people? Telling them what to do? That kind of thing?"

"I don't think, I *know* it is!" Nira's voice was getting loud, and some other clusters of students turned to look at them. "Did you know that some countries basically have slavery as part of their culture and society? Not just bigotry, but real slavery, going on from one generation to the next, rigid caste systems—"

"You guys, let's keep walking," Thomas interrupted. "I want to see the third-floor exhibit, and that security guy over there is kind of giving us the bug-eyes."

Nira looked at the guard, humphed, and said, "Well, come on then," leading them on to the next room. When she began talking again, she spoke more quietly, but still sounded angry. "Did you know that in India there is a whole group of people who are literally named 'The Untouchables,' who are not allowed to live where anyone else lives, do jobs other people do—even in school, their children aren't allowed to touch the common food or use the same plates as other children?"

"Like segregation," Thomas said, pointing to an old sign hanging on the wall that said, *Restroom—Whites Only.*

"Yes, but worse," Nira went on, "because they are literally considered lower than animals by the rest of Indian society."

Billie wondered if "A'ri" was an Indian name.

They were quiet for a few minutes as they checked out the next room, which had displays showing the different kinds of jobs slaves did on plantations in the American south. There were life-sized scenes of mannequins posed in different settings, as well as cases of artifacts that showed the tools they would have used, and the kinds of things they might have owned and kept in their cabins.

"Everyone knows slavery and racism are bad, though," she grumbled when they left that room and headed to the stairs leading to the third floor. "Why do people let it go on?"

"Everyone *doesn't* know," Nira said. "People let their own comfort and their big bank accounts make them blind to it."

"Money is power," Thomas added, huffing slightly because he was taking the stairs two at a time. "Some people will do anything to hang on to it."

"We have to fight it," Nira said as they reached the top of the stairs.

Thomas grinned at her. "Sure—we can all be *agents* for change, right Nira?" She swiped at the top of his head and he ducked, giggling, and skipped away into the next room ahead of the girls.

"What did he mean?" Billie felt like she'd missed the joke.

Nira looked at her. "*Agents*? You know, my dad? They like to tease Gaurav and me about it. Don't you get that, too?"

Billie shook her head. "I still don't get it. What—"

Nira stopped her by holding her hand up, looked to either side, then leaned close and spoke softly. "You really don't know what I'm talking about?"

Billie shook her head.

"Then I probably shouldn't tell you more," Nira cocked her head to one side, "but I will. After school—can you come over to my house?"

"I'll have to check, but probably, yeah."

"Good. Let's catch up with Thomas," she turned and walked briskly in the direction he had gone. Billie followed, pulling out her phone to text her dad about going home with Nira.

A REVELATION

"Thanks, Ma," Gaurav took a plate of tiny sandwiches from his mother and carried it to the table.

"Piano at 5:00," she said as she walked up the stairs from their basement study room. "We leave in an hour."

"My dad is picking me up in about 45 minutes, Mrs. Patel," Billie called to her.

They heard the door close above them.

"We have to explain things to Billie," Nira said to her brother. "It seems she doesn't know."

"You're kidding. They haven't told you yet?" Gaurav's eyes were wide with surprise as he stuffed a sandwich into his mouth.

"Told me what?" Billie folded her arms and began to feel nervous. "What are you guys talking about?"

"Okay," Nira pulled Billie toward a chair, pushed her down into it, and handed her a sandwich. "You know how our parents worked at the same office for a while, back when you were living in Europe?"

"Yes," Billie nodded, holding the sandwich but not eating it.

"So that means your mother and our father do the same work, or something similar, right?"

She shrugged. "I guess so."

Nira looked at Gaurav, who had finished chewing and took over talking. "For a long time, we thought our father was some kind of diplomat—you know, working for embassies because he spoke lots of languages, going from country to country. Does that sound familiar?"

"Yeah," Billie said, slowly.

Gaurav and Nira exchanged looks again.

"Our father is not a diplomat," Nira said, sitting in a chair and leaning forward, speaking softly. "He told us when I was ten."

"I was twelve," Gaurav said around another mouthful of sandwich.

"Told you what?" Billie looked from one to the other of them, frowning.

"Our father is a spy," Nira sat back and folded her arms. "And so is your mom."

"What?" Billie's voice squeaked. "Why would you—no, I mean—that's silly!"

"I'm sure your parents were going to tell you soon," Gaurav said kindly. "Kids usually get told at about our age."

"I don't believe it!" Billie almost shouted, shaking her head. "They would have told me!"

"Let me just ask you a few questions, then," Nira said, reaching for some food herself and taking a bite. "You said your mom sometimes gets a certain tone that makes you think she's keeping something from you, doesn't want to talk about something, right?"

"Well, sure, but don't all parents do that?"

"Does your mom go to lots of fancy events and have lots of meetings—does she ever have to travel away from you for a few days for work?"

"Sure, but that's just—"

"And you said you've met some ambassadors and other government official-types, they've come to your house for social events sometimes, right?"

"Well, yeah, because Mom works with them sometimes—"

"And you've moved about every two years, and now you're here, near Washington D.C., and your mom works at a military base, right?"

Billie paused before she answered. Except for staying three years in California, they had moved about every two years. And she had noticed that Mom was going up to Washington D.C. a lot during the week, and she talked about her office on base. Billie hadn't thought much about it because she was used to her mother going away for a few days now and then, having meetings and things to do in government buildings and military bases. But...

...could Nira be right? What was she doing in all those meetings, with all those government officials, anyway?

She looked at her friends. "I'm not saying I believe you, but what would it mean, if she's a spy like your dad? Is it...dangerous?"

Nira grinned and popped the rest of her sandwich into her mouth. Gaurav answered her. "Not for us, and probably not for them. Especially not here. We know other kids whose parents go to the dangerous places—war zones, unfriendly countries

—those are the kids who get scared. I think our parents keep things pretty tame."

"But it's important work, even so," Nira added. "You should probably ask your parents about it, now that you know." She stood up from her chair looking at her watch. "You can blame us, say we let the cat out of the bag."

"Well, we did," Gaurav laughed.

"Exactly," Nira was already walking up the stairs. "But if you tell them that, they won't feel like they can deny it—they'll have to come clean, since you already know about our parents working together, right?"

Billie's dad was just pulling up to the front of their house when Nira opened the front door. She waved at him and then put her hand on Billie's shoulder. "I know it's kind of a shock at first, but it's better to know."

Before walking to the waiting car, she turned to Nira. "Thanks, I think."

"No worries," Nira grinned. "See you tomorrow!"

***

"Billie, you've been pushing those peas around on your plate for ten minutes. Is something wrong? Aren't you hungry?"

Billie looked up from her plate. When she was talking to Nira and Gaurav about it, it seemed simple to go home and ask her parents about the whole spy thing. But as soon as she got in the car with Dad, her stomach started doing crazy things and she didn't know what to say. She sighed, knowing that this was the moment to ask—but how?

"Well," she put her fork down and frowned at her plate, unable to look her parents in the eye. "You worked with Nira and

Gaurav's dad back when we lived in Poland, right?" She heard the sound of silverware being put down. She sneaked a look at her parents and saw that they were looking at each other. Dad nodded to Mom, and she settled back into her chair.

"Yes, I did," her mother said simply.

"Okay," Billie took a deep breath, "well they get teased sometimes by the others—jokes about agents and secrets and stuff—and I asked them what it meant." She paused.

"Go on," Dad sounded serious, but not mad or anything. It gave Billie courage.

"So they told me." She finally lifted her eyes from her plate and looked back and forth between her parents. "They said that Mr. Patel is..." she couldn't get the word out.

"A spy?" Mom suggested.

"Mmm-hmm," Billie nodded. "And they said you are, too." She put one hand on the table, next to her plate, spreading her fingers out. "Is it true?"

Dad made a small sighing sound, and Mom smiled across the table at her. "We should have told you sooner, I guess," she was shaking her head. "We knew it was time but didn't want to overload you—what with the move and leaving Janie and everything."

"We figured once we were really all settled in here," Dad spoke up, "that'd be the time to tell you."

"Well," Billie felt her cheeks growing warm and frowned, "could you tell me now?"

Nira had been right. Billie's mom and Nira's dad worked together in the CIA. Her mother explained that their job had been to get important information that could help the government make sure other countries were following international laws. "It's kind of like being human CCTV cameras," Mom had explained. "We are supposed to get information that most people don't see, to be sure nothing bad is going on out there. That's all."

"Your mom's biggest job," Dad added, as he stood up from the table and started clearing the dishes, "is just to connect with people, talk to them, earn their trust. Then, if they find out about bad stuff happening, they tell her."

"And then I can go tell the right people to make sure it stops," Mom said. "It's really as simple as that."

"Okay," Billie said, "so why are we here, in Virginia? Are there bad people here?"

Her parents both laughed. "I'm sure Virginia has its share of bad guys," Mom said, "but I'm here so I can teach what I've learned to the people being trained to do the same job I do. And I've got some other projects going on up in D.C., too."

"She can't talk about that," Dad said in a stage whisper, winking. "It's Top Secret."

Mom rolled her eyes and handed him a dirty plate.

Billie went to bed feeling unhappy. She thought her parents should have trusted her enough to tell her the truth a lot sooner, and it made her wonder what other things she didn't know about. Before saying good night, she warned them, "This is kind of sudden, you know. I'm probably going to have lots of questions."

Her mom put her hands on Billie's shoulders and looked steadily into her eyes. "You ask anything you need to. We will be completely honest with you—including when I have to say that I can't answer a question. Okay?"

They hugged, and Billie went up to bed. She wasn't sure she'd be able to fall asleep. Her mind felt like a windstorm—

and then something new occurred to her: with her government connections, could Mom maybe help A'ri?

A'RI

Had he gone too far?

Spooning nutrient broth into his mouth, A'ri went over his last conversation with Billie for the hundredth time.

Had it been too much too soon? Should he have waited longer, given her more time to...care about him?

No. It had been a risk, sure, but his instincts told him that their friendship was solid, she believed in him, and the time was right to push things forward to the next step.

"A'ri," the Supervisor called to him from across the cantina. "You're due in barracks. No more nutrient time. Go." It sounded bored rather than angry, so A'ri took his time returning his utensils to the proper receptacles, placing his tray on the belt to be sanitized.

"Ho," the Supervisor gestured for him to come over as he headed for the door. A'ri obeyed, standing before it, all eyes respectfully downcast, arms folded behind him. "Your scores topped your class again this marking segment," it said. "Not only Processing at top efficiency for your unit, but progressing in your studies faster than the others," it tapped A'ri on the head, the signal to look up. "You'll be one of the first to be picked for Stratawork when the time comes, at this rate," it glowed a little, showing pride and approval. "A top Blank from our own natalsphere—you bring honor to us all." It leaned close, narrowing its eyes. "Don't disappoint us, will you?"

"No, Your Honor," A'ri dropped his eyes to the ground again, bowing his head lower. "It is every Blank's dream to bring honor to their natalsphere and be a model within their Strata." He felt a light push from the Supervisor's hand and turned away. He tried to walk normally, but as soon as he was out the door and out of sight he leaned against the wall, breathing as fast as if he'd just been running.

It had been a complimentary comment but being noticed for *any* reason always felt dangerous to A'ri. *What if they could tell?* He thought, feeling his heart race. *What if just saying it to Billie made a difference they could see?*

Trying to calm his breathing, he started walking again, back to his barracks. He knew there was more to engendering than merely thinking about it. Just talking about it didn't bring on the physical changes. But he'd heard stories of Blanks who couldn't control themselves, who engendered while sleeping, or when having strong feelings about something; what if the work he was doing with Billie made him lose control?

That's why it's so important to move things forward with Billie, he told himself. *That's why revealing more* now *was the right thing to do. It will pave the way, help her understand the rest. Not yet...but soon.*

The Supervisor was right, but it didn't know the half of it. A'ri had figured out a long time ago that his understanding of Strata training was light years beyond everyone else's. But he also understood that if he stood out too much, it could cause him trouble. He knew what happened to Blanks who didn't fit into their Strata, who reached beyond what they were bred for —A'ri shivered just thinking about the various punishments reserved for Misfits. Death was the *best* they could hope for.

He made sure his genius never showed, curing boredom by learning other things, in secret, during his free time. Once he decided what he wanted to do, he'd used what he learned to figure out how to use the Disruption Transmissions as transports for his own messages and programs—it was like they were hidden by the shadows of the legitimate signals sent to Earth; all he had to do was coordinate the timing and develop a tool that could separate them before they reached the Central Disruption Processing Coordinator. Since his training was mostly to prepare him and his classmates for work in Disruption and Processing Centers, he had plenty of opportunities to work on his project.

For a long time it had seemed like a game, something to challenge himself with, just for fun. Even after he'd made the Test and sent it to Earth, each time he culled a batch of results and sorted them out, finding no one suitable, it was just like another round of the game, not *real.*

But then Billie's test had come through, and suddenly it was *all* real, *everything* was possible.

He could use her to thwart what the Realm was doing to her planet. If he was successful, if his plan actually worked, it would eventually lead the way for the Blanks to stand up against the Gens, demand their rights, break free of the Strata forever.

He wasn't expecting it to happen just because of what he was planning, of course. There had been increasing trouble over the last few centuries. The Instructors and Supervisors told them it was just a few minor troublemakers, everything was under control, but A'ri knew better; he'd found files stored in hidden banks of data, reporting that uprisings were more and more common, more and more difficult to quell and keep secret.

He saw time like a long hallway, filled with doors, all of them locked. But each door had a key, and when the time was right, a civilization, a community, or sometimes a single person stood in front of one of those doors, key in hand, ready to unlock it and swing it wide.

Billie and the Earthers were his key. He just hoped he could get this door unlocked in time.

CONNECTING THE DOTS

"Look at this, guys!" Reuben jumped the last three steps to the bottom, announcing his arrival in the basement study room, waving a handful of papers over his head. He slapped some stapled pages onto the book Billie had open in front of her.

Nira leaned over to see what it was. "Oh Ru, not this again," she said.

"This is breaking news!" Reuben almost shouted. "I made copies for all of you." He started handing the packets to each of them.

"We come here to get homework done," Ben drawled, "and then get more homework!"

Thomas snickered, and Shae said, "We're all going to grow up to be astrophysicists if Ru has anything to say about it."

"Not me," Ben laughed. "I mean, no offense Ru, I totally get how cool this is. But it's never going to be my thing."

Billie was looking at the papers. She read the title of one aloud. *"If The Universe Is Expanding Faster Than It Should, We Need to be Asking Why.'* Are we supposed to be worried about this?"

Nira had already flipped to the second page. She looked up and cocked an eyebrow at Reuben. "Your Dr. M seems to think we should, doesn't he?"

"Yes!" Reuben sat down in a chair and leaned forward. "You guys, no one in power is going to take this seriously—look at how they are about global warming."

"It's too science-y, you mean," Shae said, shaking her head as she scanned the article.

"Exactly," Reuben nodded. "But if we, a bunch of kids, can understand it, then maybe there's a way to explain it to the people in government and make them do something about it."

"By what? Writing letters to our congressmen?" Thomas scoffed.

"Or congress*women*," Shae and Nira said at the same time, then high-fived each other.

"But you already said it," Ben pointed out. "Climate science is simple, and *still* people don't get it, or don't believe it. Why would things be any different with this dark stuff?"

"Also," Nira said, "this is still only theoretical. Even your Dr. Menkel says as much. If there were some kind of physical proof, maybe..."

"I'm sorry," Gaurav slapped his pencil down and pushed his math book away from him, rubbed his eyes and picked up Reuben's article. "I wasn't listening—busy trying to do *actual homework*, in case you were wondering. But I can't concentrate with all the yapping. I don't read science stuff—what's this all about?" He tossed the article on top of his book and looked around at the others.

"Yeah, bottom-line it for us, Ru," Ben said.

"Okay," Reuben stood up again, putting his hands on his hips. "Basically, it's about balance. dark matter should be consistent—there should be the same amount of it everywhere in the universe, but that's not what Dr. Menkel and other researchers are finding."

"So, like, it's missing in some places?" Shae said.

"More like it's thinner and thicker. It should be a constant, but it's not—it changes its density. In some places it seems to have almost completely disappeared, like big holes in the universe."

"Okay," Gaurav said, stifling a yawn, "I mean this with respect and everything, but so what? Isn't there a ton we don't know about this stuff? Couldn't it be that these scientists just don't understand what they're looking at?"

Reuben nodded. "Of course. But it could also point to a dangerous imbalance."

"Dangerous how?" Nira demanded.

"Well, it can change the laws of physics if the dark matter of a region shifts or disappears—and that can throw everything out of whack."

"Okay, but again...?" Gaurav let his voice trail off, holding his hands palm up in a questioning way.

"Don't you get it?" Ru grabbed his own hair with both fists and pulled, leaving it standing on end. "Maybe things like climate change aren't just about climate? Maybe even politics and social problems aren't just happening by accident! You guys," he smacked his palms on the table and leaned forward, "at the atomic level, everything is connected to everything else. There are no boundaries. The universe is a row of infinite dominoes—push one over, all the rest get moved too.”

“But Ru, even if there is something to this,” Thomas said gently, “when we can’t get people to agree about climate change—”

“—or civil rights!” Billie added

“Yeah, or any of the easy to understand, obvious changes that need to be made in the world today,” Thomas continued, “what difference do you think this stuff will make?”

“But you’re all looking at this backwards!” Reuben shoved away from the table and paced across the room, rubbing his forehead. “Let me try again: let’s say you’re sick. You get head-aches, you’re tired all the time, your joints ache and you have high blood pressure.” He looked around to make sure they were following him so far. “You go to a heart doctor for your blood pressure and get medicine for that. You go to a bone doctor for your aching joints and get medicine for that. Your family doctor gives you medicine for the headaches. And you drink tons of coffee every day for more energy.”

“Oh wait,” Ben reached out and picked up the article again. “I get it. You’re going to say that all those different things are being treated like different problems, when really, they’re different symptoms of the *same disease*.”

“Yes!” Reuben punched the air.

“Huh?” Shae was shaking her head. “But what does that have to do with—”

“What he means is that all the problems our world is facing —climate change, diseases, social injustices, overpopulation— are symptoms of an imbalance in dark matter,” Ben explained.

"Making the government pay attention to this stuff will be treating the main problem, and that could solve everything else—is that what you mean?" Billie asked.

"Exactly," Reuben nodded his head so violently, his glasses slid down his nose. He shoved them back into place. "Now you see!"

They were all quiet, until Thomas said, "Ru, it's a cool idea, but, I mean, what can *we* do about it?"

"Funding," Reuben said. "Dr. Menkel and other researchers need the funding to do the work that will prove how important this is. And that can only come from the government." He was looking at Billie now, in a way that made her feel like she was missing something important.

Before she could ask what it was, Nira said, "Ru, don't get carried away here. Even if her mother did know your Dr. M in a professional capacity, we don't know what it was for and aren't likely to find out. You know our parents won't talk to us about things like that."

Now Billie understood. Reuben was still convinced that her mother had known and worked with Dr. Menkel back when they lived in California, and he'd already figured out what it was her mother did—*probably before I did*, she thought resentfully.

"But couldn't you try again, Billie?" Reuben had clasped his hands in front of him, and she was afraid he was about to get down on one knee and beg. "Just ask her if she knew him, see if you can find out what they worked on together—at least maybe get his contact information? We could write to him ourselves and maybe get some ideas from him about how to help, if nothing else."

Mom had told her she would be completely honest, and she was welcome to ask any questions she wanted about her work. Billie nodded her head slowly. "I'll see what I can do."

Reuben jumped into the air and cheered. The others laughed or shook their heads at him. Ben stood up and stretched, saying, "I'm going to go get some sodas, and then can we please get back to the homework? I've got tons to do. Anyone else want anything from upstairs?

WANTING TO HELP

Billie sat at her desk, staring at her social studies text-book. She was supposed to be reading, but the words on the page blurred. She picked up a pencil and drummed the eraser against the page in front of her absently. Finally, she pushed her chair away from her desk and tilted her head back.

"This is pointless." She stood up, looked around her room, and decided to go downstairs. Maybe a snack would help.

She was rummaging through the pantry shelves, looking for something that sounded good, when she heard her mother in the kitchen. Grabbing a packet of crackers, she turned out the light and went to the fridge.

"Feeling peckish?" Mom asked. She was standing at the sink, a glass of water in her hand.

"Mmm," Billie said. "I can't concentrate. So...food." She opened the cheese drawer and took out a brick of cheddar.

"Here, let me slice that for you," Mom said, getting out a cutting board. "I'm having the same problem—my office feels too full of distractions today."

"For me, it's my head that's too full," Billie said, handing her the block of cheese.

"What's on your mind?"

"Well," Billie realized this might be the perfect time to make good on her promise to Ru and ask some questions, get more information about Dr. Menkel. "A bunch of things, really, but I have been wondering about..." she wasn't sure how to start.

Mom smiled down at the cheese slices she'd cut, reached for a plate to put them on. "Is it my job? Is that bothering you?"

"Not bothering me, exactly," Billie was grateful she didn't have to say it herself. "But I did want to ask you about California."

"What about it?"

"Do you remember that book I got from the library? By a scientist, Dr. Menkel, who works at Stanford?" Billie watched her mother's face carefully as she spoke. Mom just nodded, reached for the crackers and began arranging them on the plate with the cheese slices. "It seemed, before, like maybe you knew him, and I know you spent some time at Stanford when we lived there. So I was just wondering why? I mean, what does Dr. Menkel have to do with bad people, and the stuff you do?"

Mom was looking down at the plate, turning it slightly, as if admiring how it looked. Her face was carefully neutral, and Billie wondered if she was going to answer her at all. Then she picked up a cracker and a slice of cheese and took a bite. When she'd swallowed, she looked at Billie and smiled.

"I did know your Dr. Menkel. Richard and I worked together a good bit, and I got to know him pretty well. Did you know he has two poodles? The big kind, standard, one black and one white. He brings them everywhere, even into his lab when he's at work." Her eyes crinkled and she looked to Billie like she was seeing something in her mind's eye, a nice memory. "As for what he had to do with my work," her eyes focused back on Billie, "all I can tell you is that information is one of the most important things a government needs in order to make decisions. Getting the best information, from the best minds, in all kinds of different areas, is very important." She winked and smiled. "It's not like in the movies. Bad guys aren't in secret organizations we can infiltrate wearing tuxedos and evening gowns."

Billie giggled, imagining her mom in a fancy evening gown. "Okay," she said, taking her own cracker and cheese. "What are their names?" she added before taking a bite.

"Whose?"

"The poodles? Ru would like it if I told him about them."

"Oh yes, your friend who is a big fan of Richard, right? Let me see," Mom took another bite and chewed as she thought. "I'm pretty sure he calls the white one Procyon and the black one Cygnus."

"Weird names!"

Mom laughed. "I think they're named after stars."

Billie nodded. "I bet Ru will know what they mean." She reached for the plate to take back up to her room, but then said, "Mom? One more thing?"

"Sure, honey, what is it?"

"Have you ever worked on any projects that have to do with modern slavery? You know, like, human trafficking?"

Mom refilled her water glass. "That stuff has really been on your mind a lot lately, hasn't it? Ever since that field trip."

"Well, yeah, but it *should* be on our minds, right? Everyone should know about it and something should be done!" Billie's voice was rising, and she realized she sounded angry.

"Yes, of course," Mom said quietly. "You just seem to be more personally upset than I would expect. Is there," she paused and squinted, really looking hard at Billie for a few seconds, "do you know someone who's being trafficked? Is there something you should tell me, something going on that we need to act on?"

Billie looked down at her feet. She began kicking her toe into the side of the kitchen island. Could she tell Mom about A'ri? Would she be able to help?

"I just," she began, then sighed and shook her head. "Mom, it's just not right, you know? I was just wondering if it was one of the illegal things you'd worked against, and if you could tell me..." she hesitated, searching for the right words, "...what I can do about it, even though I'm just a kid?" She looked up, meeting her mother's eyes, hoping she'd found a way to ask without revealing too much.

"Human trafficking isn't something I've been involved with, though there are people, *good* people, who are working against it, trying to help. And what you can do," Mom put her glass down and reached out, tucking a stray lock of hair behind Billie's ear, "is report anything you know or hear about. To me, to a teacher or counselor at school, or even call a hotline—I know there are organizations that are set up to help with these things." She ran her thumb gently across Billie's cheek. "Okay? Does that help?"

Billie nodded. She turned to leave the kitchen, adding, "Thanks for the snack."

On her way back upstairs, she kept repeating the names of the dogs to herself, to remember them. She felt like she'd hit a dead end. She had no clue what Mom and Dr. Menkel had worked on together. 'Information' could mean anything—and why would the CIA be interested in the kind of information Dr. Menkel knew about? What does the government want with theories about dark matter?

I guess knowing that they are *interested is something*, she thought, *but it doesn't feel like enough.*

As for finding a way to help A'ri, that was a bust, too. The kinds of organizations her mom was talking about wouldn't know anything about or be able to help with what's going on in other countries—and she still didn't even know which country he was in! If mom had said she'd worked on it, maybe she could've gotten some information—even just knowing which countries were the worst ones could be an important clue. It was nice that there were "good people" working on the problem, but they hadn't saved A'ri and *his* people yet...and mysterious good guys working in secret was not the kind of thing she wanted to pin her hopes to.

At least she'd make Ru happy when she told him about the dogs—maybe he would be able to make more out of the fact that Dr. M's information was something the government wanted. And on Sunday night when she talked to A'ri, she could tell him about Ru's theory about the balance of the Universe—he loved science stuff. *It's not saving him, but maybe distracting him with interesting ideas is at least helping improve his quality of life*, she thought.

It was stormy all day Sunday. The sky was dark and it rained non-stop. Around dinner time the distant rumble of thunder echoed through the skies, and by the time Billie went to bed the night was getting split open by brilliant flashes of lightning, followed almost immediately by ear-crushing thunder. She worried that the storm might interrupt her cell service. Relief bubbled up inside her when her screen lit up at 9:13 with his name.

Hi! How are you?

Good. You?

Good. I have more info for you about DM and the guy who wrote the book on it.

Really? Great—my project is due next week.

Cool. My friend Ru...

Billie did her best to explain what Reuben had said about the problem with imbalanced dark matter in the Universe.

So, all your friends know about this stuff, too?

Ru talks about it lots. No one is as into it as he is.

But they all understand it?

Pretty much. They're really smart.

Wow—cool!

Also...

Yes?

Turns out my mom has worked with that scientist, Menkel.

No way!

Weird coincidence, right?

Yeah.

Sometimes it seems like we're all meant to know each other. Me and the others...and you, too.

I wish I could meet them. They sound great.

Maybe one day.

Maybe...

What about you. Are you safe? Everything OK?

Yes. Don't worry about me, Billie. I promise I'm fine.

But I do worry.

I'm surviving. I'm as safe as I can be. And I have you.

Promise you'll tell me if there's anything you need, anything I can do?

I promise. I'd better go now.

OK. Talk next week?

Same time next week.

Billie lay there thinking for a while before she closed her eyes. She imagined A'ri as a slave somewhere distant and cold, doomed to a miserable life with no freedom. Some place with school, she guessed—it made sense that people would want smart slaves, so they could do things for them, didn't it? She was imagining what it would be like to rescue him, bring him here, introduce him to the others.

As her thoughts wandered into sleep, she wondered if her parents would be willing to adopt him—she'd always wanted a brother, and it would be such a good thing, to give a home to a former slave, to change his life for the better...

CHAPTER

13

A'RI

Billie was going beyond his wildest expectations. This was going so well, it almost frightened him.

Her friends were key, he realized. The one boy was doing half his work for him, explaining universal balance and causation, introducing her to more complex theory and the inconsistencies in dark matter throughout the universe. All that was missing was the reason why, and only he could give her that information.

In fact, it was practically all that was left for him to do. Well, that and find some way to tell her that the reason she'll never find out which country on earth he's in, where his caste-based slavery system exists, is because it's not *on earth* at all.

And that, of course, was the really crucial part.

If she believed him, accepted the truth of his existence, then he was certain she'd believe him about everything else.

Maybe her friends could help him here, too? He tried to think of ways to pull them into their conversations, get her to tell him more about them. But he worried that it would come across as strange. The last thing he wanted was to seem like a faceless, control-seeking stranger, the very kind of unthinking human his strata training was designed to take advantage of.

He couldn't let that happen.

He'd have to trust the test he'd designed to identify humans who could help.

She'd scored a perfect 100% in every category. All the mind-sets he needed her to have in order to be likely to believe him, and to care enough to take risks for his cause, were there. Now she also cared personally about *him*—that was clear from her texts. He had to trust that who she was, along with the friend-ship they'd built, would be enough.

Friendship. It was a human concept. They had no word for it in their language because they weren't allowed to have friends. The Gen knew that if the Blanks forged bonds between them-selves, it would conflict their loyalties, cause problems. It was acceptable to be friend*ly* to each other—in fact, good manners and positive interactions were encouraged and rewarded. But no particular relationships were allowed to be pursued, ever.

Still, it happened once in a while. Two Blanks working in the same department would bond. Their friendliness would be more exaggerated with each other. They might eat sitting close by each other frequently. Physical contact between them would increase. And then, one day, one of the Supervisors would notice. They'd be watched. And if it was proven...the *best* they could hope for would be relocation. No notice, no choice. One day they simply wouldn't be there for their shift, and a new Blank would be sleeping in their bunk in the dormitory.

A'ri thought a lot about Billie's friends. He could have used his shadow programs to find their phones and poke through their photos, social media, and email. But he held back. He had a secret hope that one day he could "meet" them, and when he did he wanted it to be as honest and true as possible. He knew what Billie looked like, how humans in general appeared, and he enjoyed imagining each of them, trying to guess how their genders made them different from each other.

Most of all, he liked imagining just being one of them, accepted, a boy with friends of his own.

He shook himself. Fantasy was fine, but he had things to do. It was almost time to bring Billie into the full picture, to tell her everything, and he needed to plan it out, word for word. He needed get it *right*.

He knew he'd only have one chance. With so much riding on it, it had to be perfect. It had to *work*.

HALLOWEEN

Halloween was going to be on a Sunday.

"It's good, because it's a weekend," Thomas said when the crew was eating lunch together the week before, his mouth full of peanut butter sandwich, "but bad because we'll all have to get up for school the next morning."

"No sleeping in after sugar-bombing our brains out the night before," Ben shook his head sadly.

"What are you talking about?" Shae demanded. "You haven't been able to trick-or-treat since 4th grade!"

"Nope," Ben agreed, "but I get to eat all the leftovers that trick-or-treaters don't take home by 8:00—and I always make sure my dad buys plenty of butterfingers." He wiggled his eyebrows.

"But you're all helping with our Haunted Walk again this year, aren't you?" Nira sounded dangerous the way she asked it, like there was really no choice for any of them.

"What's the Haunted Walk?" Billie asked.

"It was Thomas's idea," Gaurav said.

"Well, kind of," Thomas shrugged. "My birthday is right before Halloween. Three years ago, my party was one of the Ghost Tours in CW we told you about."

"Thomas *loves* ghosts and spooky stuff," Shae put in, "in case you hadn't noticed."

"Anyway," Thomas continued, "they do parties sometimes, and it was all I wanted for my 8th birthday, so my parents let me have it. Afterwards we all went for pizza and ice cream."

Ben was nodding and smiling, his eyes distant. "It was pretty awesome, actually."

"You'd think anything was awesome if it involved pizza and ice cream," Nira pointed out.

"So that's your Haunted Walk? You do it on Halloween together?" Billie was confused about what Thomas's birthday party had to do with what Nira had said.

"Not exactly," Thomas went on. "After my party we were talking about how it would be cool to do something like that for trick-or-treaters on Halloween—maybe not with story-telling, but just a spooky walk for them to go on before getting their candy."

"Like a haunted house in an amusement park," Shae said, "scary scenes of Halloween creatures, people dressed in cos-tume acting creepy, fog machines…"

"And the Haunted Walk was born," Nira finished. The bell had rung for recess, so they all stood up to leave the cafeteria. "The first year it was a little simple, but it's gotten better each time, and this year it's going to be amazing."

Gaurav laughed. "Nira stalks thrift stores and garage sales all year. She's got a ton of new props."

"Where do you do it?" Billie asked as they went out the heavy double doors leading to the field and playground area.

"At our house," Gaurav said. "We made a path that goes around our house, looping through the woods in back so there are lots of shadows and places to hide and jump out and scare the kids walking through."

"Not just kids," Nira said proudly. "Last year the parents started walking through, too, and someone took pictures that ended up in the newspaper."

"Sounds great," Billie said.

"Bring your parents," Nira added. "There are always a bunch of adults hanging out inside. Some of them help out, too, but mostly it's us kids doing the Walk. The adults are there to supervise."

"She means 'party,'" Shae said with a snort.

"That, too," Nira agreed.

It turned out that it took the whole day Saturday and most of Sunday to get the Haunted Walk set up. Some of the parents helped on Saturday afternoon—Shae's and Ben's dads spent several hours setting up lighting along the path and in the woods, and a few others helped get the fog machines working, hooked up the ghost projector, and supervised the webbing-gun. But on Sunday, the final hours for pulling everything together, it was just the kids working.

"All right, it's 11:00—that means we have six hours to finish this," Nira said when everyone had arrived. She held a clipboard and was checking things off. They were all standing on the back deck, surrounded by boxes and bags. "Billie, you and Shae are in charge of hanging ghouls and bats," she pointed to several large garbage bags with labels on them. "Shae will remember where each one goes, but if you get a better idea, just do it." She turned to the boys. "Ben and Gaurav, I think you two should get to work on the last of the webs—first use up all the bagged webs, then add extra bits with the gun, if there's time. Ru and Thomas," she paused, her eyes moving across the clipboard, her lips pursed in thought. "You're on graveyard duty. Remember where we put it last year? This year we're hanging the new ghosts in the trees over there, too," she pointed with her pen at a small stack of boxes with "ghosts" written on the sides.

"Yessir!" Gaurav saluted with a chuckle.

Nira rolled her eyes and started handing people the things they'd need. "Wire, cutters, thread, string, scissors…" she looked around, "and there's the duct tape if anyone needs it." She reached for two black garbage bags. "I'll be hanging spiders." She grinned. "One of the new ones has a little motor so it can go up and down on its string, motion activated!"

Shae nodded toward the steps leading down from the deck, toward the side of the house. "Come on, Billie, we start over here."

They had to shimmy through an overgrown hedge of azalea bushes, being careful to step over wires and not accidently knock over the lights hidden inside.

"This is bigger than I thought it would be," Billie said.

"Yeah, it's a pretty big deal," Shae agreed, dropping her two bags. She pointed in both directions at the bushes and small trees that lined either side of the pathway. "This is where we hang all the bats, and a few of the ghouls," she explained. "It's the first section of the walk, so we wanted it to be spooky but not really scary yet, so we don't use much except these things and a few strobes we'll add later."

They worked together, using wire and thread to hang and pose life-sized bats just overhead, diving toward the path from the bushes and trees.

"I'm kind of surprised that Nira takes it all so seriously," Billie ventured, after a while. "It doesn't really seem like her kind of thing, you know?"

Shae laughed. "Yeah, except that organizing and telling people what to do is *exactly* her kind of thing," she said. "Also being the best at something. I don't know if you've noticed, but Nira doesn't fool around."

"No kidding," Billie laughed. "She's what my mom calls a 'force of nature.'"

"Times a thousand!"

They took a short break for lunch, which was pizza provided by the Patels, and by 3:00 Nira declared that everything was done. Together, starting from the street where trick-or-treaters would enter, the crew walked through the whole thing. Now and then they paused to fix things, move them slightly, and spread out webbing that had gotten bunched by squirrels. There was a lot of discussion about the best placement of strobes and who would stand where. Ben and Thomas debated how often the fog machines should be activated, and Nira went over general scare tactics.

When they reached the end, Nira sighed happily. "This is going to be the best one yet." She looked at her phone. "It's 3:30 now; that gives you an hour and a half to go home, get into your costumes, and get back. Be here by 5:00 even though it doesn't officially start until 5:30—every year we have some families show up early, and we want to be ready."

Billie had been assigned the role of forest zombie. She needed help to look like a decaying cadaver, and Dad spent most of an hour working on her face, applying makeup, trying to get it right. Her costume was a ragged, loose-fitting jacket, a shirt, and ripped pants she'd found at a thrift shop, made gorey with a pair of scissors and some red food coloring.

By 4:30 she was ready. The three of them drove back over to the Patel's house.

The whole thing went pretty much the way Shae had said it would. The adults took turns being outside to supervise staying inside together. Everything else was left to the kids.

Stationed around a blind corner at the beginning of the wooded section of the path, Billie jumped out, moaning and shrieking, scaring the older kids as they came along. If there were little ones, she just lurked quietly, whispering, "Happy Halloween!"

Things were slow at first, but by 6:30 the flow of trick-or-treaters was steady. The whole thing seemed magical—fog settling along the path, lit in places by strobes and colored lights, her friends hiding in the dark, moaning and cackling. The kids who walked through--sometimes in large groups, sometimes alone--seemed entranced, their laughter and shrieks mingling in the air. Toward the end of the night, as the crowds began to thin out, she heard a pair of owls calling from the trees overhead. It was spooky and thrilling, the perfect touch.

Before she knew it, it was 8:00, the official time when trick-or-treating was supposed to end. Nira came around to tell everyone it was time to stop, and the dads went around gathering the electrical equipment and unplugging lights. By 8:30 they were standing together in front of the house in the dark. With all the path lights and sounds turned off, there was no sign of the Haunted Walk at all.

"It always seems sad, when we have to shut it down," Thomas mused.

"It's the cleanup I hate," Gaurav said, scuffling his feet in pine needles.

"We'll all come over after school tomorrow to help," Ru said.

"Thanks you guys," Nira folded her arms across her chest and hunched up her shoulders against the chilly night air. "This *was* the best one ever. You guys were awesome."

They waved goodbye as they each got into cars with their parents.

Once home, Billie quickly washed off all her makeup and got ready for bed. She couldn't wait for A'ri's text chat tonight—she wanted to tell him all about their evening, in case Halloween wasn't something he was familiar with. She wanted to share the fun with him.

She got into bed right at 9:00, calling out good nights to her parents and burrowing under the covers with her phone. She only had to wait ten minutes before her screen lit up.

Hi! Happy Halloween!

> **How are you?**

**I'm great! I've got so much
to tell you!**

> **I've got something to
> tell you, too.**

CHAPTER

15

A TERRIBLE WEEK

—————————————

"I can't believe we did it all in two hours!" Thomas said, pulling a few strands of webs from his fingers. "It took days to set up!"

"It's always easier to destroy than to build," Gaurav intoned, one finger raised in the air. Then he laughed. "At least, that's what Mr. Ness always says."

"Mr. Ness?" Shae asked as she tightened the drawstrings on a bag of ghouls. "Which one is he?"

"8th grade history," Nira answered before her brother could. "I never hear the end of it, all his sayings and philosophies."

Ben shrugged. "You guys'll get it when you're in his class. Ness is awesome."

They were standing in the living room of the Patels' home, surrounded by all the boxes and bags of decorations and props they'd just unpacked and set out around the yard two days before. "Now what?" Thomas asked. "Want us to help you put this stuff in the attic?"

"No thanks," Gaurav shook his head. "Nira and I get our brother-sister bonding through the torture of going up and down, up and down, and following Dad's directions as we jigsaw everything into place up there." He put his hand to the side of his mouth and mock-whispered, "It's best if no one outside the family gets involved."

The others laughed.

"Ma has left soda and snacks for us, if you guys want to hang out?" Nira offered. They made enthusiastic noises. The teachers had been merciful the day after Halloween, no homework, so they could relax and enjoy themselves before heading home. They all started moving into the kitchen.

Billie hung back, took out her phone, and began texting.

"Billie? You coming?"

"In a minute."

By the time she joined them, they were all sitting around the table, munching on cookies and talking about the night before.

"My dad is on his way, so I'm going to wait out front for him," she said.

"Okay, sure," Nira stood up. "Is everything okay?"

Billie nodded. "I just have to get home." She looked quickly around the table at the others. "See you guys tomorrow," she said, and turned from the room, heading for the front door.

They were quiet for a moment, then Shae said, "Well that was...strange."

"Yeah," Reuben nodded. "She seemed kind of off today, you know?"

Nira shrugged. "She's probably just tired. Or maybe she's coming down with something."

It didn't take long for her dad to get there.

"How'd it go? Seems like you guys got it done pretty fast, considering how long it took to set it all up," he said.

Billie just nodded.

"Your mother and I were really impressed with the job you kids did," Dad continued. "I'm not sure what we expected, but it was...*more*." He looked sideways at her. "It's a nice group of kids. I'm glad you've found them."

Billie continued staring out the window, saying nothing.

When they got to the house, she dropped her backpack in the hallway, kicked off her shoes, and headed straight for the stairs.

"Billie, hey, dinner's ready—come to the table, okay?"

"Dad, I really don't feel well. Is it all right if I just skip dinner and go straight to bed?"

Mom came out of her office just then. "Not feeling well? Do you have a fever?"

Billie exhaled loudly. "No, I just don't feel good, and I want to go to bed, okay?" Without waiting for an answer, she turned and went up the stairs, straight into her room, and closed the door loudly behind her.

Her parents stood blinking at each other in the hallway.

"Do you know what's wrong?" her mom asked.

"No idea," her father shook his head. "Let's leave her alone for now. I'll make a plate for her, in case she gets hungry later."

Billie heard a knock at her door an hour and a half later but ignored it. Her parents came back at 9:00, quietly opened the door and peeked in. She let them think she'd fallen asleep. Her mother crossed the room and pulled the covers up around her shoulders, kissed her on the forehead, and whispered good-night. Just as she was turning away, something caught her eye. Billie opened her eyes just enough to see Mom reaching for her phone, which was on the floor beside her bed, face down. Mom picked it up and placed it on the charging pad.

When the door was closed again, Billie stuck out her arm and pushed the phone off the charger, back onto the floor.

It was a terrible week. She got a D on a math quiz, she forgot her homework three times, and by Wednesday her friends were giving her side-looks while they ate lunch. Her head hurt, she couldn't sleep, and she had a stomachache that wouldn't go away. Mom and Dad kept asking what was wrong, but she just stuck to her story that she wasn't feeling well.

How could she tell them? How could she explain in a way they'd understand?

In her mind she went around and around, facts flying across her thoughts, things making sense one second, and seeming impossible the next. Then she'd feel overwhelmed with shame —she *knew* not to trust strangers in the virtual world. But A'ri had seemed so good, and real, and like such a true friend.... she still couldn't believe she'd been wrong about him.

But if she wasn't, then everything he'd told her was true— and that was impossible, wasn't it?

And if she *had* been wrong...it made her wonder if she could really trust anyone at all. It made her want to sink into a hole and never climb out.

Friday afternoon, when the final bell rang, she picked up her backpack and headed for the busses.

"Not so fast," Reuben was suddenly there walking beside her, his arm linked through hers. "We're not taking the bus today."

"What?" Billie was confused. "We, who?"

"All of us—we're having an emergency meeting." He pulled her out of the river of kids heading toward the doors and put his hands on her shoulders. "Nira has already cleared it with all the parents; her mom is picking us up."

"Uh, okay," Billie rubbed her forehead, wishing the headache would go away, wishing she could just go home and close herself in her room again. "Where are we going?"

"CW. It's too nice a day to be inside anymore—we won't have many more days like this," Reuben sounded like her dad, Billie thought. "She's going to drop us off down by the Capitol, and we'll walk from there."

Even in her black mood, Billie could see that it was a beautiful day—which made her wish even more that she could be back in her room, in the dark, by herself. The sun was shining, the sky was dotted with fluffy white clouds, all the sticky humidity of the late autumn heat was gone—a rare perfection for southeastern Virginia. They piled out of the minivan and walked around the old Colonial Capitol building, making small talk while Billie just walked along in silence, slightly behind them. They turned down a long, tree-lined alley that she didn't recognize and continued around a big white house and several other smaller buildings. Beyond these there was another path which took them to a meadow surrounded by woods.

"Well, here we are," Nira said, her hands on her hips. They all stood there, in a kind of circle, looking at her.

Shae smiled kindly and pointed off to her left. "They made this path because there used to be a big old oak tree over there."

"Ancient, actually," Reuben added.

Shae nodded. "It was ancient when the first white people arrived. It was revered by the Powhatans who lived here."

"Even though the tree is gone now," Thomas said, "this place is still believed to be important—you know, spiritual, mystical."

"It's a place for truth," Nira said, lowering herself to the ground and crossing her legs. The others did the same, and she gestured for Billie to sit, too. "We brought you here so you can tell us what's going on."

Feeling tongue tied, Billie just looked around at them. Suddenly tears were pricking at the backs of her eyes.

"We're just worried about you," Shae said, reaching out to put a hand on her knee. "You've been so weird since Halloween. C'mon, Billie, tell us what's wrong."

Billie didn't feel the tear tracing its way down her cheek. She was numb. Finally, when no one else said more, she shook her head and mumbled, "You won't believe me if I tell you," she began. "You're going to think I'm so, so stupid..."

"We would never think that," Ru said softly. "Give us a chance. Trust us."

Trust. Billie was desperate to trust them. Maybe they could help her make sense of it all. And if not? At least she'd feel the relief of telling someone.

She pulled out her phone and told them about A'ri. The accidental wrong number, the way their friendship had grown. "He seemed like a normal kid," she explained, "you know, like one of us. Until last Sunday."

Shae nodded and smiled encouragement. "What happened?"

Billie hung her head and sighed. "He told me some things that...that seem impossible. Even crazy! And now I feel so stupid—my parents told me to be careful about stuff like this —but at the same time—"

"You said what he told you is impossible, but it sounds like you think it's for real," Ben said quietly.

Billie nodded, biting her bottom lip, holding her breath as she waited for some reaction from them.

"You'd better tell us," Reuben said.

"Here," Billie opened her text messages and scrolled for a few seconds. "Read it yourself." She handed the phone to Reuben.

"I know this is going to sound strange," Reuben read aloud, "but I promise it's the truth. I don't live on Earth. I am a citizen of a multi-system empire called The Realm, and I contacted you because I need your help." Reuben's eyes were wide, and he paused to look around at the others. Nira nodded at him, and he kept reading. "My people are enslaved by the Gen, who own us and control our lives, and we are trying to fight back. They are too powerful, though, unless..."

"Then I said, 'unless what?'" Billie spoke quietly.

"Yes," Reuben nodded, "And he went on: The Gen run everything on dark matter—but they steal it from other places in the galaxy. Right now, they're stealing it from your solar system. If you can help me cut off their supply, we might have a fighting chance here."

"He made up that story about a school research project," Billie's shoulders sagged. "It was just so I'd learn about it, so I could understand what he's talking about."

"He was preparing you," Thomas said.

"Exactly," Billie sighed. "It makes me feel so...creepy. Used, kind of. The thing is," she looked up at the others, "maybe I'm crazy, or the stupidest, most gullible person in the world, but I still want to believe him, trust him!"

"The first thing I'm thinking is, why *wouldn't* it all be true?" Gaurav said. "I mean, why would anyone troll someone with a story like this? Alien civilizations dependent on slavery and stealing from other worlds to fuel their society? How would doing this as an elaborate joke benefit anyone?"

"He never asked you for money, right?" Thomas said. "Or anything?"

"No."

"Nothing else?" Shae leaned toward her. "Think, Billie, it could be important."

Billie shook her head. "Nothing but my help with his plan."

"Help how?" Nira narrowed her eyes.

"I don't know, he didn't want to say," Billie reached out to Reuben for her phone, scrolling through the texts to the end of the conversation. "He said he knew that it was a lot to consider, and he knew that I probably didn't believe him, so he wanted me to go think about it. Before he told me more. Oh—wait," she flipped her finger over the screen. "He did tell me that he came to me on purpose. Because of a personality quiz."

"A personality quiz?" Ben had stretched out on the grass, propping himself up on his elbows. "Like one of those Buzzfeed quizzes or something?"

"Yeah," Billie nodded. "That's what he said—he created it to find people like me, who would be open to learning about him, his people...who would help him..."

"So he admitted that he designed something to get personal information about people, and targeted you," Nira's mouth had tensed into a hard line. "I don't like it."

"Here's the quiz," Billie handed her phone back to Reuben. "He said mine was the only result that even came close to what he was hoping for."

"Hmmm," Reuben had looked at the quiz, then put her phone down and steepled his fingers together.

"Do you guys..." Billie began. She couldn't finish the sentence, so tried again. "Are you guys..."

"We don't think you're crazy or stupid," Nira said firmly, "and no one is mad at you."

"If that's what you were getting at," Gaurav added, smiled at Billie. She nodded and smiled back.

"I've just felt so confused," she sighed. "I can't figure out what to believe or think about it all."

"I have an idea," Reuben said, picking up her phone again and holding it up. "Maybe a way we can check his story. Because if it's true," his eyes sparkled, "if he's the real thing..."

Thomas whistled. "That would be something. I mean *really* something."

"And if he's not," Nira said, "we need to know so we can report this whole scam to the authorities."

"Here's my idea: we all take the quiz," Reuben continued. "Sunday night, when A'ri texts you, tell him you won't do anything without us being part of it too—that's natural, right? If he's for real, and it's as important as he claims it is, then he'll have to be willing to include us in a group chat."

"I guess," Billie hesitated.

"Hey—we've got a text-to-voice simulator I used for that comp sci project last year," Gaurav exclaimed. "If we get together at our place, we can plug in one of our phones and it'll be like a conversation."

"Oh my God," Ben laughed. "How cool would it be to have a group chat with a real live alien?!"

"I wonder if he can text us some pictures of himself—I mean, wouldn't it be awesome to have pictures?" Thomas agreed, grinning.

Reuben was tapping the screen of Billie's phone. "If he's telling the truth, he'll get our test results and know a lot about us that way. Then it'll be our turn to ask him about his story. Afterward…we just have to decide if we believe him or not. Okay? What do you say?"

Billie felt relief bubbling up inside her.

"Okay," She closed her eyes and sighed. "This is so much better than trying to figure this out by myself. Thanks, you guys."

On the walk back to the Capitol building, where Mrs. Patel would pick them up, Billie texted the quiz link to the others. She was so relieved that they knew and didn't hate her or think she was nuts or stupid, she wasn't sure if she wanted to cry or laugh. For the first time all week she felt happy, and even hopeful and a little excited for talking to A'ri on Sunday.

A'RI

A'ri tapped impatiently against his workspace surface with the stylus. He was taking a risk by hurrying through the day's assignment—what if his Supervisor checked his work? He forced himself to slow down and took two deep breaths before each new step in the protocol. He only needed a small window of time to reconfigure the master schedule. There was no sense in drawing attention to himself by finishing any earlier than was absolutely essential.

He could feel his pulse racing. He felt dizzy knowing that he was so close to the end of it all, yet everything could fall apart if his next few moves weren't just right.

Trust Billie, he told himself. *You know her test results. You chose her for a reason.*

But doubt made him feel cold with worry.

Waiting for her last transmission had been one of the hardest things he had ever gone through—an entire week of not knowing what she was thinking or whether she would believe him and help him. He'd barely slept, and when he did his dreams were filled with running through doors, terrified of something catching up with him, calling for help and finding only empty rooms.

What a relief it had been to see her first message: "I want to believe you."

He'd almost begun crying when he read it. Then came her next sentence: "But I'm not sure I can."

He'd seen the half dozen new test results come in the day before, of course. They had all passed the 80% compatible threshold, and two were better than 95%. It crossed his mind that if she rejected him, he could try again with these—maybe, instead of focusing on one at a time, he could try six at once, casting a wider net in hopes of greater success?

Afterward, he realized that he should've guessed what she'd done, should have anticipated what was happening. They were forcing him to diversify his efforts, whether he wanted to or not.

Deep breaths, he told himself, concentrating on moving his stylus slowly, checking the clock. He still needed to slow things down. He put his stylus down and stretched, counted to ten, then resumed the protocol.

Although he didn't want to dwell on it, part of him was excited by what Billie had asked. He never would have suggested including her friends in their plans if she had agreed to help him. The fact that she was now refusing to help *unless* they were a part of it, and they had to be satisfied with his story too. It meant he was going to meet more Earthers, get to know them, be *himself* with them. It would not be just one person now who would know his true self, but seven! When he'd told her he wished he could meet them, he'd meant it. He had always dreamed of having friends to share things with. He'd had a taste of that with Billie, and now…maybe he'd have more friends than he ever imagined.

They have to help me, he thought, squeezing one of his hands into a knot of fingers and biting down hard on part of his mouth. *The time is now; there won't be another chance like this.*

In his usual rounds of filing things for his Supervisor that week, he'd intercepted more banned news stories. The Realm was riddled with upheaval, the number of planets where multiple Strata rebellions were happening had more than doubled, and there were reports of Blanks laying claim to identities in record numbers, defying their Gen masters and refusing to do the Stratawork, throwing the Realm economy into chaos. Certain Gen were said to have evacuated territories, continents, and in a few cases even whole planets, to escape the uprisings.

But there were also accounts of energy shortages due to the stockpiling of massive military resources. Energy was being sacrificed on a planetary level in order to build a force that could decisively crush the rebellions. A'ri knew that no matter how many ranks of Strata there were, they had no defense against the unlimited power wielded by the military. With the strength of the dark matter mining operation coming out of the Sol system, they were all but invincible.

Unless their power source could be disrupted.

Everything hinged on this one thing.

They just have to help, his mind whirred back to Billie's friends' test scores, and everything that was riding on his ability to convince them. Though their scores had varied, every single one of them had 100% alignment in one category. In all the test results he'd received, it had been rare to find Earthers with high scores in this area, and before her friends took the test, Billie was the only one who'd scored perfectly in it. But it was crucial in his search for help, and he'd ranked it the most significant factor in his testing algorithm: *empathy.* A'ri dared to hope that her friends' strong sense of identification with the plights of others would be enough to carry them through their doubts and be willing to trust him...and to help.

A bell sounded, indicating the shift was nearly over, warning the Blanks that they must finish or be penalized. With a few swift strokes, A'ri dashed through all but the last task left to him. Then, checking first to be certain the Supervisor was occupied with other Blanks' last-minute problems as he'd hoped, he used the backdoor he'd created to access the master schedule, and rearranged the shifts.

When the final bell sounded, he had just completed the day's assignment. He allowed himself a small smile before composing himself as a model Blank should. With pleasant neutrality on his face, he shuffled unhurriedly with his work-mates toward the cantina.

He'd had to assign himself a double shift a little further down in the schedule to make it work, but the schedule now showed he was free at the time Billie had told him, so he could communicate with all the Earthers together.

All he had to do now was wait.

In two more Earth days, he would know if they were going to help him, or if everything was lost.

THE MEETING

Everyone was there by 11:00. That's the time they picked, because it wasn't early enough to make their parents question them, but would give them plenty of time for A'ri, plus getting the weekend homework done.

Shae was the last to arrive, and she ran down the stairs breathlessly.

"Sorry I'm late guys," she panted. "Nira, your mom told me to tell you that lunch is in the fridge, and we can bring it down here whenever we want."

"You're not late," Nira smiled, "and thanks. Gaurav was just about to go over the set-up for us." She turned to her brother.

"Right," he said. "It's all over here." He led them to the far end of the room, where chairs and beanbags had been set up in front of an old television screen.

"Where did you get this?" Ben said, bending over to look behind it.

"A garage sale. It was all part of my computer science project last year," Gaurav explained. "I wanted to create an app that would translate speech to text." He turned to Billie and held out his hand. "A'ri is going to text on your phone, right?"

She nodded, handing it to him. "And I brought the adapter for you, too." She dug around in her jeans pocket, bringing out a short white cord and giving it to him, too. "Your app is going to mean we can talk, and it'll go into the phone as text?"

"Not only that," Gaurav knelt on the floor in front of the screen and began plugging wires into what looked like a hard drive, checking to make sure they were connected to the screen in back. "This little box here," he picked up a small, square piece of equipment that was sitting beside the hard drive, "will allow us to hear A'ri's texted words aloud, too." He grinned at the others. "That's why this is better than the usual text dictation that's standard on our phones. It goes both ways."

"So you could do text chatting like a real conversation?" Thomas got down on the floor and picked up the speaker, looking it over.

"Exactly," Gaurav said, plugging Billie's phone in. "And we'll also see everything on the screen here," he punched a button on the side of the old flat screen, it hummed and went blue. "I thought that'd be a good way to keep an eye on auto-correct...and get around any mispronunciations my app might have."

Billie's eyes were wide. "This is amazing, Gaurav. I hope you got an A on your project."

"B+ actually," he said. "There were some, uh, problems. But don't worry, I've worked them out."

Reuben was reaching into his backpack. He pulled out papers that he started handing around.

"Ru, we don't have time for another article," Ben snorted.

"These are notes," Reuben corrected him, "you know, a place to write down what you're thinking as we go...and I've taken the liberty of typing up some questions we might want to ask...just to be sure we don't forget them."

They each took a sheet from him and read over his questions.

"Ooh, tough one right up front," Nira muttered, nodding. "I like it. I would add one about why he chose Billie—what was it about her test results that made him reach out to her?""Perfect! Write it down!" Reuben handed her a pen, and then gave one to each of the others as well. "Just write down anything you think of."

They were quiet a while longer, some of them scribbling on their papers. Then Nira said, "It's almost time."

Billie felt her stomach drop. "I'm so nervous," she said in a wavery voice.

Her phone pinged. Gaurav tapped the screen, and suddenly the television showed the notification: *Message from A'RI*. He looked at her, and she nodded. He tapped her phone screen again, and a text bubble sprang into view on the right side of the screen. Half a second later they heard, "Hello? This is A'ri. Are you there?"

"A'ri? Th-this is Billie," as she spoke, her words appeared in a text bubble on the left side of the screen. "We're all here, together."

"Okay," the voice Gaurav had given the app sounded digital and a little off, like it was unsure about what it was saying. "Hello, everyone, it's nice to meet you."

"A'ri, this is Reuben," Ru scooted a little closer to the phone and spoke loudly. "We have some questions we'd like to ask you, if you don't mind."

"That's what I'm here for. I'll tell you anything you want to know."

"Okay, our first question is: how can you prove to us that what you told Billie is true, that you really *are* an alien?"

"I thought you might ask something like that," came the reply.

"If we can't believe you," Nira said, "nothing else really matters, right? Oh—this is Nira talking."

"Nira. Thank you for taking my test. I know you really care about doing the right thing." There was a pause before A'ri continued. "I saw all of your test results. Billie makes good choices in her friends." They exchanged looks, and Billie smiled. A'ri continued. "I will give you something to prove that what I'm telling you is true. But first I think it's important to explain some things."

For the next ten minutes, the six of them simply listened as A'ri told them about the history of his people and the structure of his society.

"A'ri wait a minute," Ben finally interrupted. "Let me get this straight: you guys have been around for almost a billion years, and you still have slavery? You haven't, like, outgrown it?"

"That was Ben," Nira jumped in, "and this is Nira speaking now. It sounds like what you're telling us is that your empire—"

"The Realm."

"Yes, The Realm has been so successful in continuing the system of slavery that it was built on, that it's become almost programmed into your people?"

"Not programmed, bred. We Blanks are bred for qualities that make us good workers, servants, slaves. We're bred for different jobs throughout the three star systems, from manual labor to technological and energy systems. And although we're used to it, because it's been this way for so long, it's not what we want, and more and more are trying to rebel."

Ben leaned forward. "What was it you said about getting to choose....?"

"Gender," A'ri said. "Unlike you Earthers, we are not born with a particular gender. When we grow up, we can take on either gender, stay neutral, and even switch back and forth."

"Like those frogs we studied in biology last year," Gaurav whispered. Ben and Thomas nodded.

"But *you* are not allowed to choose," Billie said.

"Blanks are forced to remain neutral, unless selected for reproductive roles; then we are told what to be, based on the needs of the natalsphere we are servicing."

"That's horrible!" Nira said angrily.

"Reuben here. I understand Blanks get no choice, but your owners?"

"The Gen can do whatever they want," A'ri said.

"I just don't get how your people haven't gotten past this kind of thing. I mean," Ben looked around at his friends and shrugged, "we did, and we're not nearly as advanced as you guys."

"That's where dark matter comes into the story," A'ri said.

He explained that the discovery of how dark matter could be used as a source of energy, more powerful than any other planetary resource, meant unlimited power to those who had control over the mining industry.

"The Gen, obviously," Nira said ruefully.

"Exactly. We Blanks never stood a chance once dark matter was discovered. We were stuck being the property of the Gen. But it was all more complicated than they realized, way back at the beginning.

"At first, they siphoned off their own dark matter, right in their home solar system. But soon they realized that it was making a mess of everything—from planetary orbits to ecosystem destruction on the homeworlds."

"How can dark matter make a difference in ecosystems?" Thomas asked.

"Remember your Dr. Menkel!" Reuben raised his finger in the air. "Dark matter is everywhere, around and in everything—*everything*. So if it's being destroyed in one place, that's going to affect things all over the system, maybe even further."

"This is Shae." She leaned toward the phone, a look of concentration on her face. "It's like ripples in a pond, isn't it A'ri? Drop a pebble in on one side, and the ripples spread out across the entire thing."

"Yes, that's it exactly. To avoid hurting their own system, the early Gen started looking outside for sources, to other systems in the galaxy. That worked pretty well, but after a while they noticed that they could get more dark matter from the systems where planets were inhabited."

"How come?" Billie asked.

"It took them a while, but they finally figured it out: the more dark matter they took from a system that had planets with civilizations, the more self-destructive those civilizations became. There were more conflicts, less social stability. The environment grew less balanced, resource scarcity increased, and so on. *And the more self-destructive a civilization became, the easier it was to harvest the dark matter from the system.* It tripled their output."

"Let me guess: the Gen got richer and even more powerful?" Gaurav asked.

"Yes, and they expanded into two more star systems. But to keep everything going, they had to keep harvesting dark matter at that same rate. The early explorers tried creating chaos in unpopulated systems by throwing off orbits, drawing asteroids into the path of planets to cause destruction, that kind of thing. It worked to a small degree, but nothing was as good as the disruption of a civilization. Eventually they stopped even trying, because it was too expensive and didn't get the results they wanted. From then on, they targeted systems with civilizations on purpose, and an entire industry developed around causing problems for the civilizations ahead of time, to kind of loosen up the dark matter."

"So dark matter works like erosion," Shae suggested. "When some soil gets washed away, the rest becomes looser, and the roots are unprotected. The plants get weak and die, and without their root systems even more soil washes away... kind of a bad cycle of destruction. Is that right?"

"Pretty much," A'ri said.

"Wow," Ben exhaled.

"It can take centuries to get a system to maximum output of dark matter," A'ri continued, "and sometimes they even have to build up the civilization to make it happen."

"So, what...they teach cave men to read and write? That kind of thing?" Thomas asked.

"Something like that," A'ri responded. "It's like planting seeds: we have a whole Intervention Department that figures out how to give primitive cultures ideas, philosophies, traditions, technology and beliefs that'll make it easier for the Gen to turn them against themselves and tear themselves apart in the end."

"Hmm," Nira said. "The more advanced a civilization is, the easier it is for the Gen to create problems? Of course they'd want to hurry things along on more primitive planets."

"Did that happen here?" Thomas asked. His voice sounded small, and they all looked up at each other, realizing the implications of what he was asking. "Did the Gen 'plant' human civilization on Earth?"

Reuben's eyes grew wide. "UFOs!" He gasped

"Pyramids. The Iron Age. The printing press. Electricity. Radio." Shae ticked off different technological leaps on her fingers. "Were any of them actually ours?"

"Do you really want to know?" A'ri asked.

They looked at each other in silence. Then Gaurav said simply, "Yes."

The screen was empty and the speaker silent for a few seconds before A'ri responded.

"Most of your major technological leaps were introduced by the Gen," he said. "Nothing you wouldn't have eventually figured out yourselves—technology has to make sense to the people using it. But you got it faster because of The Realm's interference."

Gaurav let out a long, low whistle.

"This is...deep," Thomas said, taking his glasses off and rubbing his eyes.

"Exactly," A'ri's computer generated voice said. "And now with your advanced technology, your planet is just the way the Gen like it: they can do everything via transmissions, never leave their own systems. It's more efficient and less expensive."

"And today, the state of the world...it just keeps getting worse, doesn't it?" Ben's voice shook slightly.

"All the conflict, wars, over-population, environmental destruction, political strife and everything going wrong, getting more horrible..." Nira added.

"That comes from the Gen." A'ri's words glowed on the television screen. "It's what I was bred and trained to do."

"Oh my gosh--bots!" Reuben shouted.

"Fake news!" Thomas exclaimed.

"Memes and misinformation—maybe even social media in general?" Ben asked.

"Yes. All of it. And the more dark matter they take, the worse things get. That's how it works." There was silence in the room. After a few moments, he spoke again. "I'm asking you to help me stop it. For your planet, your people, and for mine. Because if we can cut off the power supply coming from your solar system, it will not only save your civilization, but it could help the Blanks change things here, too."

"If it's true, we don't really have a choice, do we?" Nira said to the others in a hushed voice that the phone didn't pick up.

Reuben cleared his throat and leaned forward.

"This is Reuben. We understand what you're saying, but we need proof that what you're telling us is true," he said. "You said you had something for us?"

***

At 12:00, they disconnected. The screen still showed the last few words they'd exchanged.

I have to go in a moment. I can't risk longer. Please, check those addresses. You'll see I'm telling you the truth.

We will, we promise.

Time is running out here. Please, hurry.

We will. Stay safe.

Thank you.

They sat staring at the screen.

Ben broke the silence.

"That was…." He left the sentence unfinished.

Thomas turned his note paper over. It was blank. He stared at it, shaking his head slightly. "If it's all true…"

"That's what we have to find out," Nira stood, stretching her arms above her head. "You have it all written down, Ru?"

Reuben nodded, waving a piece of paper in the air.

In order to prove that his story was true, A'ri had given them a series of web addresses. They were electronic "back doors" into multinational corporations and government agencies around the world. He'd explained that his natalsphere was made up of Blanks who were trained to gather information from every available source. Their data collections would enable other Blanks to plant "destabilization vehicles" in various places. He hoped that by going to these secret web locations and seeing that he had real information because of his "job," they would know that he was telling the truth.

They all stared down at the list of URLs on Reuben's paper.

"We'll have to be careful," Nira said quietly. "We don't want any of these places to be able to trace us. That could be really dangerous."

"These are Dark Web addresses," Gaurav said.

"How do you know?" Billie asked.

"See how they end? '.onion' instead of '.com'."

"What does that mean?" Shae frowned. "Is it related to dark matter?"

"No," Gaurav smiled, "though it's kind of a funny coincidence, isn't it? The Dark Web is a place that makes it a lot harder to trace what people are doing, so criminals like to use it for illegal activity."

"But also governments, intelligence agencies...anyone who wants extra security." Ben added. "It's good for us, actually, because it'll make what we do untraceable, too."

"But maybe we should still use a public server, or something?" Thomas said.

"I know just the thing!" Reuben said, folding his arms across his chest and looking around at them all. "And we can do it tomorrow—we'll have our answer before Billie's usual Sunday night chat with A'ri."

As they went upstairs Ben said, "Hey, I just thought of something."

"What?" Thomas asked.

"Remember how A'ri said that they tried messing up un-inhabited systems too, with things like asteroids, and it just didn't work as well?"

"So?" Nira said.

"Well," he paused at the top of the stairs, hands on his hips looking down at the others, "maybe this is crazy, but the Gen have been around, doing this stuff, for like a bazillion years, right? And 65 million years ago, there was no civilization on this planet that could be used..."

From the bottom of the stairs, Shae sucked in some air and her eyes grew wide. "And then a meteor came and changed the direction of evolution and then...we came along."

They all looked at each other.

"The sooner we figure out if all this is true, the better," Gaurav said quietly.

ALL IN

Billie pedaled slowly as she biked home. Suddenly she turned sharply to the left, heading for the colonial section of town rather than going past the nearby college campus. She wanted time to think.

She heard a bell chiming, and knew it was from the clock tower in the old church. It was 2:00. She and the others had been at the library for two hours, checking the web addresses A'ri had given them, figuring out whether they could believe him or not.

The November sunlight was bright and clear, and Billie squinted as she rode. The trees along the streets still had most of their leaves, all reds and golds now, and she thought about how pretty it all was. She felt protective of her new home—she didn't want it to be destroyed by an alien civilization just so they could have the power they needed to run their empire.

But that's what'll happen, ultimately, she thought, *if we don't help A'ri.*

Telling their parents they had a school project to work on, they had all met at the library when it opened at noon. Reuben brought his notes from their conversation the day before and an old laptop. He led them to one of the conference tables in the general work room.

"I thought this would be the safest thing," he explained in a hushed voice while the clunky old laptop booted up. "When I went to that STEM camp last summer, one of my projects was to fix up an old laptop—so it works, but it's not associated with anyone's accounts or anything. It's going to be slow, but I thought safety was more important than speed."

"And using the library's wifi also protects us," Gaurav said, pulling a chair around and sitting in it. "Anything we do could be traced here, potentially, but not to any of us specifically."

"Exactly," Reuben nodded, his fingers tapping the keys to login to the wifi. "To save time, I did download the browser we'll need to access the Dark Web," he said. "We just have to cross our fingers that there's no gate-keeping software here that'll flag us for using it." He clicked some more buttons, selecting the program he needed, entering a password, and the others watched silently. After a while, a window opened on the screen. On it was a picture of an onion, and the words, *Welcome to Tor Browser.* "We're in!" Reuben whispered. He handed some papers to Thomas, who was sitting closest to him. "Start reading me web addresses. Let's see what A'ri wanted to show us."

Billie pulled off the road and laid her bike on its side. She was at the wide meadow behind the old courthouse, where they brought her that first time. She lowered herself onto the grass and lay back. The sun felt warm on her face. She watched the clouds overhead move and change shape, letting her mind wander over the different websites they'd visited.

Reuben had been right about his computer being slow. It was frustrating, but each new Dark Web page was worth the wait. A'ri had given them access to secret websites belonging to every intelligence agency they'd ever heard of: NSA, FBI, CIA, MI6, and even Chinese, Korean and Russian agencies (if their guesses based on the alphabets and characters were correct). There were also addresses that appeared to be internal security hubs for major corporations. They found themselves looking at a site for an international bank and what they guessed was a Saudi Arabian oil company. (The Arabic script was incomprehensible, but Ben recognized the insignia and said it was something called Aramco, which he'd done a report on for social studies once.) They even ended up on the internal executive communications site for Apple.

"This is incredible," Thomas kept whispering.

"Is there any way he could have faked this stuff?" Shae said when they got to the end of the list. "I really don't know much about the Dark Web, but people can make fake websites on the *regular* web if they want to. It happens a lot on TV."

"This would be a pretty elaborate hoax, if he did," Ben was shaking his head. "I mean, we can click right through all the links and actually see data and internal memos," he reached over and took the mouse from Reuben, demonstrating with the bank website they were on. "Look at this! And we can do this with every one of these. That would have taken months to construct. Why would he do that?"

"I agree," Reuben said, taking the mouse back, "but there may be one way to be certain."

"How?"

Reuben looked at Nira and Gaurav, then at Billie. "Let's look at the CIA page again."

The three of them locked eyes, then nodded at Reuben. "Okay."

Thomas read the address aloud again, and a couple of minutes later the CIA page had loaded. Reuben moved the selector to a tiny search window at the bottom of the screen. "All right, guys?" He looked questioningly at them.

Billie nodded. She already believed in A'ri, but she knew that the more certain they could all be, the better. "Go ahead," she said.

Reuben started typing.

The details in the personnel files he pulled up were a complete surprise to Billie. She understood why the CIA would keep records about her mother's work, but there were pages and pages about her and her father, too: every job her father had ever worked, copies of contracts, dates of unemployment, and more personal things too, like medical records, including details about the time she had her tonsils removed, and when she broke her arm skiing.

Nira and Gaurav also seemed stunned when they saw the files attached to their father's personnel records. Birth certificates, photos, a log of their mother's involvement in local political races and social organizations—and a lengthy entry about Nira and the essay contest she won in 5th grade, complete with newspaper reports and emails from the Governor's office.

Reuben closed the tab and logged out. He took his hands off the keyboard and rested them in his lap. Looking around at the others, wide-eyed and silent around him, he asked, "So, what do you guys think?"

Ben was shaking his head. "After that last stuff? I mean—this is no fake."

"I agree," Thomas said, handing the papers back to Reuben.

"I'm a believer," Shae grinned. "And—do you guys realize what this means?"

Nira pushed her chair away from the table and stood up quickly. "I think we're done here. Ru, shut that down. Meet us outside." She turned on her heel and marched to the nearest exit.

Leaving the library, she led the way across the parking lot, stopping beside the fountain which burbled and splashed in the middle of a large public garden, about fifty feet away. When Reuben caught up with the rest of them, backpack slung over his shoulder, she put her hands on her hips and said, "Shae is right. We need to be absolutely clear about what this means."

"It means we believe A'ri," Thomas said, shrugging. "I think we got that."

"No," Nira shook her head. "I mean the big picture. Look you guys, deciding that we believe A'ri isn't that simple. It means we *have* to help. Because we know the fate of our planet, our solar system, even the whole universe is at stake. There's no going back from this--helping is our *moral imperative*."

Gaurav groaned. "Come on, Nira, don't be so dramatic. I mean, you're right, but...let's just enjoy this, okay?" He grinned, and playfully punched her in the shoulder. "No 'fate of the universe' and 'moral imperative' stuff. I mean, can't it just be epically cool that we know a real live alien?" Nira raised another finger and opened her mouth, but he cut her off before she could speak, patting her arm gently. "Okay, okay. Let's just focus on helping A'ri." He looked around at the others, who were nodding.

"We get it, this is big," Shae smiled at Nira. "But if we think about all that...well, it's almost *too* big. Let's just show up for A'ri and do the next right thing."

Nira seemed to relax. "Okay. The next right thing."

They all turned to look at Billie.

She knew the next step was hers to take. Tonight, when A'ri texted, she would tell him that they'd followed the addresses, they believed him, and they wanted to do whatever was necessary to make things right.

She closed her eyes and relaxed her face, trying to think only about the feel of sunlight on her skin, the cool breeze blowing over her, the prickly grass beneath her fingers.

She was happy that she'd been right about A'ri.

At the same time, it was scary to think that everything he'd told them was true—because now finding a way to fix things, to stop the Realm and help A'ri start a revolution, really mattered. It wasn't science fiction, make-believe, or wishful thinking. It was real, it affected billions—maybe trillions? —of lives, and even if Nira was being over-dramatic, she was right: it all rested on their shoulders.

But they were just a bunch of kids. Who would listen to them? How could they really do anything that would make a difference?

His text came at 9:17.

You there?

Yes.

OK. Good. Did you guys look at the stuff I gave you?

Yes. We're in. It was amazing.

I'm so relieved! Thank you!

Me too. I mean, I'm glad we can all work together. Trust each other. Be friends.

Me too. You have no idea how much this means to me.

What do we do now? What comes next?

I don't have much time tonight, so I'm going to send attachment with instructions. You'll show the others?

Of course.

There it is—got it.

Don't print at home, ok?

Why?

Trust me—just don't. You will understand when you read it.

OK. @ library tomorrow after school good?

Yes.

Can I ask you a question?

Sure.

Have you seen me?

What do you mean?

Like pictures. From my phone or...someplace else.

Yes.

How do I look to you?

Humans are different from us.

Ugly

Not ugly. Different. We're trained to accept the ways alien races look different from us.

I like your eyes.

Really?

Yes. They show me who you are. Good inside.

Thanks. Do you think we'll ever meet? In person?

Our atmospheres aren't the same.

So probably not then.

Probably not.

But maybe I can see you? One day?

Maybe one day. If things work out. Gotta go now. Bye—and thank you!

A'RI

Things were getting tense. Everything felt uncertain, on edge. The quiet murmur of pleasant, work-day conversations he was used to hearing in the barracks and cantina when they were off-shift had been replaced with a frightened, uneasy silence. Supervisors had short tempers, inflicting punishments for the smallest infractions of rules and procedures—things they used to ignore, or give only a mild correction notice, now were being penalized with extra shiftwork, reduced nourishment rations, and more and more often physical punishment.

They all watched in shock one day in the Cantina as a Supervisor beat a Blank into unconsciousness for spilling nutrient broth. Its name was C'un, and A'ri had known it his whole life. Always slower than the others and a little clumsy, it was generally expected that C'un would end up in the Lifework Corps, the rest of its life spent cleaning and maintaining Gen homes and living spaces. It wasn't enviable stratawork.

Lifework Blanks spent their lives in shamed anonymity, the lowest order of domestic slaves. They were never called upon for procreation, and there was no possibility of promotion. Their lives were usually shorter than other Blanks. As a result, C'un's rank in their natalsphere was low, but this brutal public punishment for a simple accident he probably couldn't help sent a clear message to the rest: no mistakes, no irregularities would be tolerated.

A'ri was extra careful to draw no attention to himself. He made sure his numbers were accurate, but only in the top 10% of his coworkers, with an occasional dip, just to make him look more normal. He resisted the temptation to delve into the hidden files of news events from throughout the Realm until he was certain of safety.

Then he understood why things had changed so dramatically.

Three systems had gone into full rebellion in the past week. All Gen were expelled or killed, and organized Blanks were demanding the planets be recognized as autonomous homeworlds.

The reports were generally dismissive of these demands, expressing easy confidence in the Realm Forces to eradicate them and return order to those planets soon. One transmission stated,

Once the weapons are fully loaded and charged, thanks to the increasingly productive mining operation in the Sol system and the willing sacrifice of Gen citizens throughout the Realm who are donating so many of their energy shares, Realm citizens should soon see a peaceful resolution of these problems, and a return to the High Order, with Blanks once again compliant and in their rightful place.

Just before he closed out, a small headline caught A'ri's eye. It was a brief report about the Blanks' unified collective. It was mocking and condescending but skimming over it A'ri got one new piece of information: the Blanks had a name for themselves, "Oh'hani," which meant "The People" in one of the original planetary dialects spoken on the ancestral homeworld. Their leader had engendered as female, and called herself "M'ira," which meant simply, "she."

A'ri memorized everything he read. Especially the information about when the Realm Forces would be ready. He knew the estimates were probably overly optimistic and added a little more time to his guess about how long they had: six months. He was grateful for the condescending confidence of the Realm leadership, who seemed in no great hurry because they felt assured of total victory. Why rush into a battle, when you can take your time to ensure your forces are so massively equipped that a single broad stroke will decide things once and for all?

As he closed out of the secret files and covered his digital tracks, he went over everything in his head. He hoped it was enough time for Billie and the others to set things in motion, and for the Earthers to make a difference.

It was their only hope.

MIDNIGHT MISSION.

"Do you believe in Fate?" Reuben peered over the top of his glasses at Billie.

"Huh?"

"You know, like, that some things are *meant* to happen?" He shoved his glasses up his nose and jabbed a finger at the papers she'd just printed out on the library printer. He'd been the only one who could meet her at the library after school. "Because I don't. I mean, I don't think I do. But isn't it kind of amazing that the thing that brought us together—Dr. Menkel and his book on dark matter—is at the center of everything we're doing here? And your mom's connection to him is—"

"Sssh, Ru!" Billie made a shushing motion with her hand. "Keep it down—we don't want the whole library to hear you." Ever since she saw the data files on her family's lives, she'd felt a sense of paranoia about being watched and overheard.

"Okay sorry," he leaned closer to her and lowered his voice again. "But do you know what I mean?"

"It *is* a little spooky," she admitted. "I just can't believe I have to break into my mom's computer. I see why A'ri told me not to print this at home! If she catches me, I'm going to be in so much trouble..."

"Yes, but we know what's at stake," Reuben said. "We have to try. Once you get into her computer, you can give A'ri access —and then you're done."

"Yeah," Billie sighed, "until the next part." She skimmed over the second and third pages of instruction. "I'm just not sure how we're going to pull it off..."

Reuben was scratching his chin and nodding. "We need a lot of brains to figure this out. I'll see how soon we can get the whole crew together. We need everyone to see this."

"In the meantime, I'll get to work on my part," Billie blew out a heavy sigh and ran her hand through her hair. "It feels impossible."

"I'm sure you'll figure something out," Reuben patted her on the shoulder energetically. "A'ri picked you for a reason. Trust him."

"Thanks," Billie gathered the papers and stood up. "Let me know when the meeting is. Hopefully I'll have it done by then."

It was almost 4:30. Billie biked straight home, hoping to get there before Mom got home from work so she could take a look at her office and form some kind of plan.

A'ri's instructions were clear: first she had to log in to her mother's work computer. He had information to help her with that. He had provided her with a code that she should type into the desktop search window after logging in that would open a way for A'ri to remotely access the files stored on the computer.

There's a possibility that what I need isn't stored there, but kept on an external drive or memory stick somewhere, he'd written. *If that's the case, you'll have to find it and plug it in for me.*

Billie groaned inwardly. How could she be sure to have enough time to do all this? She knew that her mom usually left her briefcase on her desk, with her computer inside. But how could she keep her away from her office long enough to get in there and do everything A'ri wanted?

Billie parked her bike inside their garage, hung her helmet on the handlebars, and went in through the garage door. Her mother's car wasn't there, and she could hear Dad downstairs in the basement, a rhythmic swishing sound telling her he was working out on the treadmill. Without even stopping long enough to take off her backpack, she headed straight for the office.

The door was closed, but not locked. She twisted the door-knob and winced as it made a slight creaking sound. She waited, heard nothing, and pushed the door open.

It was a very organized place. Framed maps were hung around the walls. Behind the desk was a floor-to-ceiling bookshelf filled with books and knick-knacks from around the world. Billie felt overwhelmed—everything she looked at seemed like it might be important. She shook her head.

"Okay, focus," she whispered under her breath. "If the files aren't on the computer, I'll have to find them. Where would she hide a thumb drive?"

Billie went around behind the desk, and gently began open-ing drawers. They were filled with normal things: pens, paper clips, post-it pads, envelopes, a stapler. She remembered seeing a movie where there had been a false bottom in a drawer, so she knocked quietly on the bottom of each one, even though she wasn't sure what she was listening for. They all sounded like normal wood bottoms, nothing hollow or strange. She reached into the back of each drawer, feeling around for something like a thumb drive or memory stick, but found nothing. The last drawer she looked in, on the bottom left side of the desk, had a lot of hanging files in it. She looked through them, finding nothing but papers. She was about to close the drawer when she remembered to check the very back. She pushed the files forward, but all she found was a copy of Dr. Menkel's book. She recognized it because it had the same cover as the one she'd gotten from the library.

No wonder Mom looked at me funny when she saw me with that book, Billie thought. *She must've thought I'd gotten this one out of her desk!*

She picked up the book and opened the front cover. There was a note scrawled in very messy handwriting. She stared at it for a few seconds, trying to make sense of it.

> *"The music of the spheres*
> *echoes and reverberates in*
> *the great cosmic symphony.*
> *May your work be the har-*
> *monious descant! ~RM 149"*

Clearly, Billie thought, Dr. M had known her mother and approved of whatever it was she was working on. She wondered if somehow the two of them knew something about what was going on with A'ri's world and the dark matter mining, when she heard a sound that made her freeze.

"I'm home! Hey, where is everybody?"

As quickly and silently as she could, Billie closed the book, put it back in the drawer, moved the files back into place and pushed it closed. Checking to see if she'd left anything out of place, she tiptoed back to the door, pulled it open called, "I'm up here! Be down in a minute!" to cover the squeaky sound of the doorknob as she pulled the door closed. Dashing across the hall to her own bedroom, she dropped her backpack on her bed, shrugged off her sweater, and rushed downstairs. She ran into Mom on her way up the stairs.

"Hi Mom!" She said breathlessly.

"Well hi there," Mom smiled, reaching out for a one-armed hug. "Doing homework?"

"Oh, yeah, but I'm ready for a break," Billie hugged her back and continued down the stairs. "I'm gonna go ask Dad when dinner is."

"I have a few things to wrap up for work—come get me when it's ready, will you?"

"Sure!" Billie hoped she didn't look as guilty as she felt.

She watched Mom carefully during dinner and throughout their evening together but didn't see any sign that she was upset or suspicious. By bedtime she was pretty sure Mom had no idea she'd been in her office and gone through her desk.

She also had a plan for getting into her computer.

The conversation at the dinner table had been all about the workday. She had funny stories about an important meeting she'd had that day. She also told them about an email from someone she and Dad used to know, and the two of them spent a long time discussing him.

When they'd finished eating Billie cleared the table and left them, still talking about their old friends and the email while they sipped their wine. She had a little homework to do, but before she went to her room she peeked into the office. The door was ajar. She pushed it open just enough to see that, as usual, the briefcase was sitting on the desk, the top open and a soft glow emanating from inside—Billie knew that meant the computer was there, ready for her to pay a visit.

In her room, she set her alarm for 2:00 am. She figured her parents would be sound asleep by that time. Next, following A'ri's instructions, she texted him a message, telling him what time she was going to attempt to access the computer. She hoped she was giving him enough warning, but if not, there was nothing she could do about it. If this didn't work…

One thing at a time, she told herself.

She didn't need the alarm—sleep was impossible. Her mind was whirling, thinking through all the things that could possibly happen, all the "*what if's.*" At midnight she got up and put her ear to the door, listening. She heard nothing. She waited until just before 2:00, then tiptoed to the bathroom to get a drink of water. On the way she listened at her parents' bedroom door and heard snoring.

Now was the time.

She hurried to her room, grabbed her phone and the instructions from A'ri, and went to the office.

As silently as she could, she opened the door. The only light in the room came from streetlights outside, but she could see everything she needed to see. She went right to the open briefcase. Mom had closed her laptop before she went to bed, so Billie opened it and waited for the screen to light up and cue her for login codes.

You will only have three chances to login correctly, A'ri wrote in his directions. *If you don't get it by the third try, you'll be locked out and so will your mom the next time she tries to login. I'm sure of all the gateway codes, but the password is guesswork.* He'd then listed six codes, numbered in the order she should enter them, followed by the three most likely passwords he'd figured out.

Billie looked at them. Sweat prickled at the back of her neck.

The first login window popped up, and she entered the identification code A'ri had given her. It worked. Each of the next windows accepted the codes A'ri had provided. All six of them worked, each time passing her on to a new submission window. Finally, it prompted her to enter a password. She tried the first one. She could tell it was a combination of names and birth dates—hers, her dad's, and what she was pretty sure was her grandma's middle name. The computer showed a spinning circle for a few seconds, and then gave an error message.

She had to re-enter all six gateway codes again before it allowed her to try the second password suggestion listed on her instructions. It didn't work either.

She had one more chance to get it right.

She looked at the third password. This was just a series of numbers. She stared at them for a while, until she recognized them as their old zip code followed by their phone number here, ending with her birth date, with some symbols mixed in.

It felt wrong to her.

What would Mom use for her password?

Billie guessed that she'd use a combination of words and numbers, more like the first one A'ri suggested. She thought about Mom, her sense of humor, the things she liked and cared about.

Suddenly she had an idea. On the drive out from California, they had a running joke that they were a corporation whose business was sampling waffle houses in every state. They named themselves Marobengle Enterprises, a combination of all of their names, and Dad signed the check at every waffle house as if he were the CEO.

She typed *3Marobengles!*

The computer showed its spinning circle again, and then flashed **Welcome Back!**

She was in!

Feeling anxious, she got up and tiptoed to the door to listen. The house was still quiet, no sound of movement, so she returned to the desk and clicked on the search box. Reading carefully from the printed instructions, she typed in the code A'ri specified and hit *Enter*. The screen dimmed, flickered a few times, and then a text box appeared in the center of the screen.

> *You did it, we're in! Now give me a minute to look around in the files here and see if I can find what we need.*

She clapped her hands silently and kept her eyes on the screen, waiting for A'ri's next text. It took five minutes, and she was beginning to worry, before he wrote again.

This is bad. It's not here. Nothing—no contact information, no records files, no meeting notes, nothing. You're going to have to see if you can find it somewhere else...

She looked around, feeling hopeless. There was nothing in any of the drawers, she knew, and she didn't see anything on her mom's shelves that could be a storage place for computer things, or even a hiding place for secret stuff. As a last resort she reached down and felt on the underside of the center desk drawer, hoping she might find something taped there...but there was nothing. She put the cursor in the text box and typed.

A'ri, there's nothing around here. I checked earlier--the drawers are just full of paper stuff, no computer things.

Nothing anywhere that could hide something small?

The only thing I found was
a copy of Dr. M's book. He
wrote in it for Mom, you
can tell they knew each
other and--

She remembered something strange about the inscription.

Hang on a sec--let me check something--

Quietly she pulled the bottom left drawer open, pushed all the hanging files out of the way, reached in and took out the book. She looked again at the inscription. He'd signed it "RM 149." *What was the 149 for?* She looked closer, and it seemed to her that the numbers were written in a different handwriting, clearer, larger than the rest. She thought for a minute, then started flipping the pages until she got to page 149—and there, in the center of the book, a rectangular hole had been carved out, inside of which sat a small thumb drive.

Suppressing an excited squeal, Billie grabbed it and plugged it into the drive on the side of the laptop.

Found something. See if
this has what you're looking
for.

She waited another 4 minutes, listening for sounds and hoping that it was the right drive, with everything A'ri needed, until finally he texted back.

BINGO! I've uploaded everything. Put it away and shut down. I'll be in touch soon and we can set phase two in motion. THANK YOU, BILLIE!!!

Heart pounding wildly—excitement? fear? —she quickly ejected the drive, put it back in the book and replaced it in the drawer, arranging the files the way they'd been originally. She cringed as the drawer closed with a soft thud, freezing in place to see if the sound had awakened her parents. Everything stayed silent. She quickly logged out of the computer. Just in case, she grabbed a Kleenex from the box on the corner of the desk and swiped it back and forth over the keyboard before closing it, the way she'd seen it done on TV. She didn't know if her mom would check for fingerprints, but better safe than sorry. She wiped the top and edges of the laptop, too, and made her way silently out the door and back to her own room.

MAKING PLANS

The next day in English class, the teacher handed out packets to each student as they walked through the door.

"Pop quiz!"

Most kids groaned. Billie sighed as she reached for her pencil—she'd read the latest chapter, but she was so tired after the night before, she wasn't sure she remembered anything.

After about ten minutes, Nira got up to sharpen her pencil. As she walked past Billie's desk, she dropped a folded piece of paper on top of her quiz paper. Billie quickly grabbed the paper and pulled it into her lap, glancing over her shoulder to see if the teacher had noticed. When she was sure no one was looking, she opened it.

> **My house, after school.**
> **Ma will pick us all up,**
> **can drive you home after.**

Billie caught Nira's eye and nodded once, then turned back to her quiz.

She'd brought A'ri's instructions with her to school. It was too risky to leave them anywhere that her parents might find them, keeping them with her seemed the safest thing. Now she could show them to everyone after school and they would work out what to do next.

***

"So that's it," Thomas said. "That's all we have to do? Hey, no problem!" He grinned ironically at the others.

"We have to try," Nira said firmly.

"I don't understand why he needs us to be there," Ben said, shaking his head. "I mean, he got whatever he needed from your mom's files, right?" He looked at Billie. "He's going to email his 'truth bombs' anyway. Why do we have to be involved?"

"The human element?" Gaurav suggested. "Maybe he thinks the whole thing will be more convincing if a bunch of kids show up and get behind this. You know, it'll be harder to ignore us—we're cute!"

Reuben waved his arms in the air over the papers. "No, no, no," he said. "I mean, yes, that's part of it. But don't you see? More than anything else, we're his insurance policy."

The others looked blankly at him.

"How's that?" Shae asked.

"As eye-witnesses, we provide corroboration for what's going to happen—six witnesses who can stand up to anyone who might want to deny it," Reuben explained. "Not only that, but with two of us videoing the whole thing, we can *prove* we're telling the truth!"

"And A'ri can make videos go viral," Billie reminded them. "That's kind of his specialty, isn't it?"

There was quiet as they thought about the possibilities. Then Ben said, "So I just want to really understand this—big picture, okay?" He walked away from the table where they'd laid out the printed instructions and started pacing around the room. "A'ri is going to tell the top astrophysicists of the world the truth about his people, their dark matter mining, and how it's messing up our world—"

"The whole system, really," Reuben interrupted.

"Yes, okay," Ben nodded, "and he's hoping that by telling all of them at once, enough of them will be convinced to go to their governments and demand the measures necessary to … what? Stop the Realm from mining our dark matter?"

"Yeah," Thomas said. "A'ri gives the same, verifiable facts and proofs to all the scientists. Even if only some of them act on it…when it turns out to be true, the ones who didn't act on it will look really bad; they'll figure this out, so they'll *all* have to get on board and do something, right away."

Gaurav sighed loudly, shaking his head. "This is huge. I almost don't believe it, even though I do." He gestured toward the papers lying on the table in front of them. "How are we going to do to this, then?"

Nira pulled one of the pages toward herself. "First we have to figure out how to get to the convention."

"How perfect is it that there's an Astrophysicists Convention this week in D.C.?" Reuben shook his head. He looked at Billie. "See? Fate. I may become a believer."

"Well, we know it's not *really* a convention," Shae said. "A'ri told us it's just a cover for the CIA to recruit more scientists from other countries—because they're looking to expand the work Billie's mom was doing with Dr. Menkel."

"They must be on to something," Gaurav muttered. "What did A'ri find in those files?" he asked Billie.

She shrugged. "He never said. He only told me he got what he needed, and he'd be back in touch soon."

"Focus you guys," Nira snapped her fingers. "The 'convention' opening day is this Friday—that's three days from now. How are we going to get there? How do we get out of school? We need a plan!"

"I might have an idea," Ben said, hesitantly. "Elijah's home from college for Thanksgiving Break. I might be able to talk him into driving us."

"I don't know..." Nira frowned. "Elijah has always seemed sort of..."

"Irresponsible," Shae finished her sentence.

The others nodded, but Ben shook his head. "Yeah, I know, but that could work for us. He's always telling me I'm too serious. Maybe if he thought he was helping me be less of a good student, he'd be willing to help."

"It's worth a try," Reuben said. "Can you talk to him tonight?" Ben nodded. "If he says no, or you decide it's not going to work with him, we'll still have a couple days to figure something else out."

"Let's assume Elijah will do it," Gaurav said. "The Welcome Session, where A'ri wants us to be, begins at noon. It's a 2-hour drive to D. C.—"

"Figure three, for traffic and parking," Shae interrupted.

"Right," Gaurav nodded. "We'd need to leave by 9:00 at the latest, and we should be back by 4:00. What about school? And our parents?"

Nira smiled, looking around the table at the others. "That's the easy part," she said. "Leave that to me."

A'RI

He barely slept any more. Any time he was scheduled for rest periods in the barracks, he just lay there going over every detail, every angle, searching for a flaw, something forgotten or overlooked.

He couldn't find any.

When he did doze off, he dreamed of Earth, saw Billie and her friends, watched events unfold like clockwork, until—inevitably something would go wrong, and he'd wake up with a start, his pulse racing.

And so he'd start over from the beginning, thinking through everything all over again.

The information package—what Billie was calling his "truth bomb"—had all the necessary components: data to fill the gaps on what the Earthers had begun to understand about dark matter and coordinates where they could observe things for themselves. Especially important was the tech filter tool he'd designed. This would enable the Earthers to detect the Realm's transmission interventions and see how complete the manipulation of their world actually was.

And, of course, the final piece, the thing he hoped would ensure their cooperation: the partial formula for creating dark matter energy converters.

That was the part he'd needed Billie's mother's files for. It was all based on a hunch he'd had, reading between the lines of Dr. Menkel's most recent research and looking at the timing of his communications with her. A'ri could read the dark web files himself, and knew that officially their collaboration had been routine, an intelligence officer gathering information from a top scientist, just in case it proved useful to her country.

What was important was their *unofficial* work together, which he hadn't been certain of until Billie found her mother's notes and encrypted correspondence. That gave him what he hoped was the perfect motivation for the Earthers: the promise that, if they helped him, he could elaborate on Dr. Menkel's secret work, saving them decades, perhaps generations of research. He could show them how to use their own dark matter to solve their planet's growing energy and resource crises.

Safely.

That was the key.

The Realm's DM Conversion industry didn't bother with safety. They guzzled dark matter, wasted it. But A'ri had learned about the secret research of a small group of progressive scientists who were trying to get the Realm to switch to a different system, one which recycled the wasted DM, regenerating it. The proposal was ingenious. A'ri could see right away that it would ultimately eradicate the need to find new sources of dark matter. They would be able to mine their own system without causing the catastrophic imbalances, eliminating the need to elsewhere.

The scale on which the change would have to be made, and the expense of it, meant that these Gen scientists were mostly ignored by the Realm leadership. Their proposals were met with ridicule and dark, threatening hints about what would happen to them if they continued advocating for the system to change. A'ri understood why: an empire built on slave labor that enabled them to consume energy resources as if they were endless had no interest in changing its ways, especially when such change would mean they'd have to sacrifice their own comfort and, ultimately, power.

But A'ri thought if he used those scientists' research to teach Earthers to harvest their own DM responsibly, safely, he could help them recover even more quickly from the centuries of disruption the Realm had caused. He just hoped that offering the promise of a source of endless power, exponentially more effective than any source used by the Earthers now, one that was completely clean and renewable, would be enough to convince first the scientists, and then their world leaders, to do as he asked.

For now, he would only give them enough to convince them it *could* be done. That was the final push to get them to work with him: letting them know he would only share the rest of the formulae they needed once they'd accomplished *his* goal. Quid pro quo.

Everything was ready. He'd done everything he could do. Now he had to wait, trust his friends to do their part, and watch what happened.

WASHINGTON D.C.

Friday morning Billie got up at the usual time and got ready for school. She was loading her breakfast dishes in the dishwasher when her dad walked into the kitchen.

"Well thank you very much," he said with a chuckle. "Is this a special occasion, or are you an alien body-snatcher in my daughter's place?"

Billie groaned. "Come on Dad, I'm not that bad."

"With breakfast dishes?" He scratched his chin with comic exaggeration. "Yes, yes you are..."

"Okay, ha ha," Billie closed the dishwasher and turned around. "Don't forget that I'm going to hang out in CW with the guys after school today."

"Yup," Dad nodded. "Shoot me a text when you're ready to be picked up."

"Ben's older brother is driving us," Billie was glad to be able to tell the truth, at least a little bit. "I'll be home before dark."

"Check. Dinner is just us tonight, so if you want to order a pizza or something—"

"How come? Where's Mom?"

"She's got some work stuff," Dad picked up a sponge and began wiping the counter down. "She'll be home late."

Billie frowned. She hoped her mother wasn't going to be somewhere in town. She might decide to come looking for her in CW between meetings. "Okay," she said over her shoulder as she reached for her backpack and hooked it around one shoulder. "Gotta get going, bus'll be here in a minute. See you later!"

"Have a great day!"

It had turned cold, the lingering mildness of Virginia's autumn replaced with real winter weather. Billie watched her breath puff out in misty clouds as she stood at the bus stop, waiting with the neighborhood kids. It felt weird doing normal things like waiting for the bus on a day when, if things went well, the entire world could change. She knew it was important to act as if nothing were different, so she asked one of the other kids about the science homework and pretended to listen to his answer.

She went through the motions of a typical school morning, feeling detached, almost frozen inside herself, until the bell rang at the end of Homeroom. From there she went to her first class, Math, where she suddenly felt like she'd been zapped with energy. She could hardly sit still. Her stomach felt crazy. She was sweating. She asked to go to the drinking fountain twice in the first fifteen minutes.

At 8:50 the classroom phone rang. Ms. Cramble answered it, looking around the room until she found Billie. When she hung up, she said, "Billie, you're wanted in the office. They said to bring your things."

Shoving her unopened math book back in her pack, Billie hurried out of the room.

The others were already in the front office, waiting for her.

"There she is!" A tall young man with a shaved head exclaimed. He turned to the secretary and smiled. Billie noticed that he had deep dimples in both cheeks. "Mrs. Berger, it has been so nice to see you again. I can hardly believe it's been ten years since I went here—you don't look a day older!"

Billie watched the school secretary, who was usually grumpy and almost never smiled, blush and pout back at him.

"Oh, go on," she said, batting the air. "You may have been a handful back when you went here, Elijah Morris, but you've grown into quite a young man!" She turned to glare at Ben. "I only hope your little brother can learn from your good example."

"You take care, Mrs. B!" he said, winking at her as he turned away and led them all out the front doors of the school.

"Smooth, bro," Ben punched his brother in the arm. "You had old Bergermeister eating out of the palm of your hand!"

Elijah chuckled. "Ya gotta learn how to sweet talk 'em, Ben, if you want to get around 'em." He led them across the parking lot to a green station wagon. "The getaway car!" He clicked a button on his keychain, unlocking the doors.

They all laughed as they scooted across the seats and buckled their seatbelts.

"What did you say to get us out of class?" Thomas asked as they were pulling out of the parking lot.

"I didn't *say* anything," Elijah said. "But I *implied* plenty."

"Is that why you called us first?" Gaurav asked.

"Yup. Everyone knows your family biz," Elijah turned onto the main street and headed toward the freeway. "If you guys get picked up from school, it doesn't take much to make an old gossip like Mrs. B jump to conclusions."

"But didn't she want to know about the rest of us?" Billie asked.

"I just hinted that it was an event on base that all your families were invited to," Elijah said. "That's all it took."

Nira leaned forward in her seat. "Good. The timing has worked out perfectly. We all got entered as "present" in home-room attendance, and because you signed us out, our absences from the rest of the day's classes will be marked excused."

"No robo-calls home," Shae nodded at Nira.

"Back in my day, we just ditched school—no planning in-volved," Elijah said, looking over at his brother. "You guys are so organized, doesn't it kinda take all the fun out of it?"

"Nope," Ben grinned back at him.

"I guess it takes all kinds," Elijah shrugged. "Skipping school to go to a national astrophysics convention in D.C. wouldn't have been my idea of a good time when I was a kid!" He settled back into his seat as he turned the steering wheel. "Okay, de-linquent nerds, we just turned onto I95. We have an Easy Pass and a carful, so we can use the HOV lane. Should hit D.C. in about two and a half hours."

Ben turned around to face the others, who were crowded into the back seat. "Here we go," he said.

The others looked solemnly at each other. Reuben cracked a broad smile and put his arms across the shoulders of Billie and Gaurav, who were sitting on either side of him.

"Don't worry, guys," he said, "we got this!"

Nira shook her head and rolled her eyes. She pulled her backpack into her lap and unzipped a side pocket. Pulling out a pile of note cards, she started handing them around. "We might as well use the drive time to review our jobs and be sure we are clear on what to do."

"Your jobs?" Elijah asked, glancing in the rearview mirror at the faces in the back seat. "I thought this was just a convention about science stuff?"

"Oh, it is," Ben explained, taking the card Nira held out to him. "But there are presentations and stuff, and we're giving one…you know, future scientists of America, that kind of thing?"

Elijah shook his head as if he were sad but grinned at his little brother. "Whatever, dude. Whatever."

They arrived in the city slightly ahead of schedule, just before 11:30. Nira asked Elijah to drop them off at the Air and Space Museum.

"We'll meet you back here around 2:00," she said as she climbed out of the car. "Ben will text you if we are running late."

"Cool. I'll be here." Elijah nodded, then looked at his little brother. "Good luck, bro. Knock the brainiacs dead!" He pulled away, tapping twice on the horn and waving as he left them, standing together at the edge of the National Mall, just across from the museum.

"Ok," Nira looked at her phone. "We have thirty-five minutes before it starts, and I think we want to get there ten minutes ahead of time."

"I'm going to need time to find my way to the tech booth," Gaurav said, frowning.

"We need to change first," Nira said. "Do you all have your clothes?" They nodded. "Good. We can change in the bathrooms. I'll give you each your ID card to clip on, and then we can figure out where the conference room is."

They climbed the stairs toward the front doors of the museum.

"It's a cool idea, holding this thing at the actual Air and Space Museum," Thomas said.

"Yeah," Ben agreed. "Who knew there were conference rooms hidden inside this place? I thought it was all just...museum."

They went through security, passed the information desks, and found the closest bathrooms. Nira had instructed everyone to bring something to change into that would look "like stuff adults would think kids might wear if they were in a young scientists club."

Billie exchanged her t-shirt for a button-down blouse and pulled a blue cardigan out to put over it. She'd worn leggings to school, but brought a long, knit skirt.

"That's perfect!" Nira exclaimed when she came out of her stall. "Now put these on," she handed Billie a pair of glasses, "and the look is complete. Don't worry, they're fake—just plastic lenses, you'll be able to see just fine. Since you and Ru are giving the presentation, I thought the glasses would be a good idea."

Billie looked at herself in the bathroom mirror. "I can really rock the granny look," she laughed.

"What about me?" Shae stood beside her, wearing a tunic dress with a blazer. The colors clashed badly. "Color-blind nerd girl? Is it too much?"

"No," Nira said, "there's one in every crowd."

They laughed.

"You look perfect, though," Billie said, brushing a wrinkle out of the back of Nira's jacket. "Definitely the President of the club."

"Well," Nira said, tucking her tailored blouse into her slacks and pulling the jacket into place, "I thought I'd better try to look really professional."

"Let's go see what Ru's wearing!" They hurried out of the bathroom and found the boys waiting for them by a bench, near the escalators.

"You guys look...amazing!" Nira said, her eyes wide.

"You sound so surprised," Gaurav said with a smirk. "What did you expect, fashion faux pas?"

Billie looked them over. Gaurav, Thomas and Ben were wearing button down shirts with clean, tan trousers, and all three of them had ties. Gaurav also had a button-down sweater vest on, making him look like a very young college professor. Reuben had gone a different route. He wore a black turtleneck and black pants, and carried a gray cardigan over his arm.

"Very nice," Shae complimented them.

"That's more than we can say for you..." Thomas sniggered, reaching out to grab the front of her blazer, then letting it fall. "I think you took the anti-social nerd girl thing a little too far."

"Hmph," Shae pretended to be offended. "I'll have you know brains matter more than fashion!"

"All right, you guys," Nira hefted her backpack and started rummaging around inside. "Here are your ID badges. Clip them to your shirts."

"You have a lamination machine?" Ben asked, clipping his badge in place.

"Left over from Ma's political campaign work," Gaurav explained. "Pretty good, eh?"

"Yeah," Thomas was squinting down at his badge. "'Commonwealth League of Future Astrophysicists.' Ugh--did you use our yearbook pictures for these? Mine is awful!"

"We just cropped pictures from our phones," Nira said, shouldering her backpack again. "Come on, it's almost time. Let's go find the convention."

MOM

"The CLFA?" The middle-aged woman behind the welcome table flipped through the papers on her clipboard. "I wasn't aware we were hosting any student organizations. Are you sure you're not lost?" She looked up at them, over the rim of her glasses, reminding Billie of the librarian. "This convention is for *actual* scientists, children."

"I think you'll find our names on the list," Nira said with a sniff, lifting her chin and gazing down her nose at the woman. "Start with me. Patel, Nira."

Sighing, the woman ran her finger down the page, flipped to the second, then the third, slowly reading names. "Oh!" She said, surprise on her face. "There you are. And—" she lifted the clipboard closer to her face, reading across the page, "it does say you're with the CLFA." She smiled up at Nira. "No one told me there'd be students, but what a wonderful opportunity for you all to experience the world of *real* science!" She reached for a stamp and ink pad, and after checking for each of their names, stamped the backs of their hands and handed them a pamphlet. "The stamp will allow you to come and go easily. Here is the full weekend schedule of events and presentations."

"Thank you, ma'am," Ben was the last to get his stamp. "Have a nice day. I hope we'll see you again." He smiled warmly, showing off the same dimples as his brother.

"Oh!" The woman looked startled, and her cheeks grew pink. "I'm with the group from Berkeley. You can come by our table during the gallery walk tomorrow morning—I'm in charge of the morning session."

As they walked away from the table toward the double doors leading to the auditorium, Gaurav elbowed Ben in the ribs.

"Practicing Elijah's moves?" he muttered.

"Hey, you never know when you might need an ally," Ben shrugged, grinning. "Am I right?"

"Just don't get carried away," Nira said, absently. They walked down a short hallway, which ended in a large room filled with rows of chairs all facing a stage with a screen and a podium. There were easily five hundred seats in all, but only about two hundred people, still milling around, talking, waiting to take their seats.

"Over there," Thomas whispered, pointing to a section of seats toward the back on the side of the room where no one else was sitting. They moved all the way to the far end of the row, closest to the wall and furthest from any other people.

"This seems good," Shae said. "We'll look like shy kids if we stay back here—that seems believable."

"All right," Nira said. "Eight minutes to go." Just then the lights in the auditorium flashed three times. "There's the warning for people to take their seats," she looked around at the others. "Everyone know what to do?"

Gaurav stood up. "I've got to get moving." He squinted up at the back wall. Keeping his hand low he pointed up at a small, square window near the ceiling. "That must be the tech booth."

"Keep your phones on silent," Nira said, nodding at him.

"I'll let you know if I run into any problems." He grinned at the others. "See you all at the rendezvous!"

They watched him shuffle back down the row, turn up the aisle, and disappear out a side exit.

"I guess we'd better get into position, too," Thomas said, looking at Shae. She pressed her lips together and nodded.

"I'll take left, you take right?"

"Got it."

They stood and moved to the main aisle. Thomas walked halfway down the length of the auditorium, then cut right through an empty row of seats, choosing one in the middle with a good view of the stage. Shae went to the back of the room, keeping away from the adults, going to the back corner where she stood in the shadows.

Billie, Ben, Reuben and Nira watched as their friends got into place, then turned back to each other. The house lights flickered again.

"Two-minute warning," Reuben said.

Nira flipped open the program pamphlet. "There we are," she pointed to a spot midway down the page. "'12:45--The Future Is In Our Hands,' CLFA, Hamilton Middle School'. He's put us right before the first break, at the end of the first hour of presentations." She raised an eyebrow at Billie. "A'ri has a sense of humor, doesn't he?"

"I guess he'd have to, to survive," Reuben said, frowning. "I sure hope this works."

"Yeah," Billie agreed. "For him, and for all of us." Her stomach fluttered nervously. She tried not to think about getting on the stage in front of all those scientists—even knowing Reuben would be at her side didn't help.

The lights lowered and everyone settled into their seats. A woman walked across the stage toward the podium, and people started clapping.

"I'm going to text A'ri," Billie whispered, looking down at her phone. "Our presentation is about 45 minutes away. That should give him time to get his stuff ready."

"Billie," Ben hissed.

"Just a minute," she breathed, her thumbs flying.

"Billie," Reuben's whisper was urgent. "Look!"

Billie looked up from her phone to see what they were fussing about. On the stage, the woman had reached the podium and was adjusting the microphone.

"Welcome, everyone, welcome to the first ever international gathering of Astrophysicists. Thank you all for coming. We couldn't be more proud to be hosting you in our nation's capitol, here in the Smithsonian's Air and Space Museum, which pays homage to everything that has led to this moment, and all the amazing work you continue to do in your efforts to advance mankind's understanding of the universe we share."

Billie stared, her mouth hanging open. Her stomach seemed to turn inside out and her heart started pounding. "Oh no," she gasped. "Mom!"

THE TRUTH BOMB

"What're we gonna do?" Ben's whisper sounded panicky. "We can't let your mom see you—I don't think fake glasses will fool her!"

"Shh," Nira held a finger to her lips. "First of all, we can't panic." She turned to scan the audience of adults, who were all facing the stage, listening to what Billie's mom was saying. "There's a chance she won't recognize any of the rest of us," she whispered when there was a momentary burst of applause. "I'll go up with Ru, Billie can just stay back here, with you, out of sight." She looked around, then pointed to an exit sign in the corner behind them, at the back of the room. "When you two leave, go out that way, instead of the main doors, just to be safe."

Billie nodded, then slumped down in her chair. "Dad said Mom would be late tonight. I just assumed she was in meetings around town…I never thought…"

"It doesn't change anything," Nira whispered firmly.

"We should've expected this," Reuben was shaking his head. "After all, we knew she was the contact person for Dr. M— it would almost be strange if she *wasn't* here," he craned his neck to look out over the audience, then relaxed, shaking his head. "I haven't spotted him yet, but he must be here."

The audience applauded again, and Billie realized her mother was leaving the stage. A group of three people were climbing the stairs and heading toward the podium in her place.

"This is the first group presenting," Nira said, reading her program. "They're from Harvard."

The presentation lasted ten minutes. Billie found most of what they said difficult to follow.

"I didn't think it'd be this hard to understand them, after all the stuff I've learned from A'ri," she whispered to Reuben.

"They were awful," Reuben said a little too loudly. Nira shushed him. "Sorry. But they were. Nothing original, no intellectual creativity."

The next group was from Switzerland, and the one that followed was Japanese.

At 12:30, the fourth group mounted the stage.

"Yes!" Reuben shouted, his voice thankfully covered by applause. "Look! It's him! It's him!"

"Calm down, Ru," Ben laughed, patting him on the shoulder. "Don't be such a fanboy."

The fourth group was three scientists from Stanford, including Dr. Menkel. Once on stage they introduced themselves, then took turns giving brief speeches summarizing their work.

Dr. M went last, narrating a video that showed animated illustrations of his latest research. Reuben sat on the edge of his seat throughout the entire thing, his hands clasped together. When the Stanford group finished, Billie and Nira had to grab his arms to keep him from giving a standing ovation.

As the next group went up to the stage, Ben leaned over to Reuben. "So, not disappointing? He's everything you thought he'd be?"

Reuben snorted. "He couldn't have been anything else."

Nira rolled her eyes, and Billie giggled.

Just then their phones lit up.

"It's Gaurav," Billie whispered. "He's in the booth."

Reuben looked across at Nira. "Perfect timing," his eyes were dancing. "We're next."

Another group of American scientists took the stage. Billie suddenly found it hard to pay attention to anything they said. She kept having to look down at her program to see who they were. From MIT, they gave a brief spoken introduction, then showed a video which explained their work.

When the audience started clapping and the MIT group made their way down the stage stairs, Nira and Reuben stood up.

"Wish us luck," Nira said.

"May the Force be with you," Ben gave them a thumbs-up, and Reuben laughed.

"I'm texting A'ri now," Billie lifted her phone from her lap. "See you at the rendezvous."

She and Ben watched their friends walk down the aisle, climb the stage stairs, and walk across to the podium. Billie looked around, trying to find her mother. She wanted to see her face, see if she showed any sign of recognition.

Ben was watching her and guessed what she was looking for. "It doesn't really matter now, does it?" he whispered. "As long as she doesn't see you—"

Billie nodded. "I know," she sighed. "It just makes me nervous."

Ben just nodded and raised his phone. He was supposed to video the whole thing. Billie looked to where Thomas was sitting. She could just make out his phone screen held up, aimed at the stage. She assumed Shae was back in her corner, doing the same.

The applause died down as Nira adjusted the microphone to a height that she and Reuben could speak into.

"Ladies and gentlemen, esteemed scientists of our beloved planet, thank you for giving us the opportunity to join you and speak to you today," Nira said. Billie thought she sounded amazingly calm, and wondered if, underneath it all, her heart was racing, too? "Unlike the rest of you, we do not have a research program to tell you about, but we do have important, in fact *vital*, information to share with you today." She stepped aside, and Reuben moved in front of the mic.

"We realize that we are mere children," he began, "and our lives are lacking the years of study, research, and accomplishments you all have achieved. We are here today because we know that yours are the finest minds in the world, the most able to comprehend complex and difficult-to-understand data." He raised his hand and pointed at the tech window, nodding, and the screen lit up with the first slide of their presentation. Leaning close to the microphone, Reuben lowered his voice dramatically. "Prepare to overcome disbelief. The world will never be the same for you again."

A'RI

He was sitting at his shiftwork console, manipulating the latest batch of data on his Surface, when the alert came through. He'd rigged his projector to stutter when there was a notification from Earth, so when the image before him flickered slightly, he knew the time had come.

Scanning his break code card onto his console monitor device, Ari paused the activity on his Surface, got up, and headed for the exit.

"What is the nature of your excuse?" One of the new Supervisors stopped him at the door.

"Biological demands, Sir," A'ri made sure his eyes were properly downcast, his voice pleasantly neutral, betraying no urgency, nothing out of the ordinary.

The Supervisor stood silently for a few moments. A'ri knew it wanted him to sweat—they were all doing that these days, threatening to take away privileges that the Blanks had long taken for granted, basic daily operations. Just to keep them quiet, frightened, obedient.

"Go," the Supervisor growled at last, as if taking a bathroom break were the most unreasonable excuse it had ever heard. "Be quick about it."

A'ri mumbled, trying to sound frightened and respectful all at once, and shuffled out into the hall. As soon as he was certain he was out of sight, he changed direction and headed toward the disused storage room where he'd set up a remote work Surface. He could never have kept it there long-term. He only needed it to be available for the final, crucial transmissions for a short window of time. After that, either everything would change and secrecy would no longer be a problem, or...

He didn't allow himself to think of the alternative.

Punching the code into the lock pad on the door, he slipped inside quickly, closing the door behind him. The device was hidden behind shelving and storage units at the back of the room, but in the dark he could see the purple glow. He hurried over to it and read Billie's text.

We're here. Things are about to start. We're up in 45 minutes. Gaurav is working on the tech angle. Ready?

He did some quick calculations in his head—given the time-lapse in transmitting, and how long it took him to get to the storage room, he estimated they now had thirty minutes. He checked his work space—everything was there, ready. All he had to do was send it at the right moment.

Ready.

While he waited, he sent a notice of illness from the Medical Center to his shift Supervisor. He needed more time than a normal bio break would account for, so he decided to fake illness to make sure no one went searching for him. Once he was done in here, he'd go straight to the MC and claim to feel ill. He just hoped no one would compare the time stamp on the notice to his Supervisor to when he actually checked into the MC.

This is Gaurav. I'm in the booth.

A'ri checked the time: ten Earth minutes. The moments went by so slowly. Then:

It's Billie—they're on stage, it's time!

A'ri took a deep breath.

Thank you. All of you. No matter what happens, thank you.

He sent the text, then used his stylus to move a much more lengthy transmission onto the outgoing stream, so that every scientist attending the convention would, in a matter of moments, find a new email in their inboxes—the first overview of everything he had to tell them.

The second email he would arrange to send in three hours.

He hoped it was enough time for them to be ready for the next set of data, proofs and other information—the 'truth bomb.' He needed them to be receptive, willing to question everything they thought they knew, and ready to hear about The Realm's role in their history, their daily lives. He couldn't afford to give them more than three hours—now that things were happening, they had to happen fast.

Exhaling slowly, he dimmed the surface and hid his work. He would only use this secret place a little while longer—first to send the 'truth bomb,' then to receive and deal with whatever response it brought about.

And, of course, for as long as possible, to communicate with Billie and the others. No matter what happened, he wasn't ready to lose them.

"My friends," he said aloud to himself as he shut the storage room door and turned toward the MC. "*My friends.*"

A CLEAN GETAWAY

Nira and Reuben had been up there for eight minutes.

Billie kept her eyes on the audience the whole time.

At first there were friendly chuckles—especially after the way Ru started things off. Billie noticed that no one was looking down at their phones, though—she hoped that was a good sign. Once the slide show started, the adults seemed genuinely interested. A'ri had done a fantastic job of weaving together what was already known about dark matter with historical facts and statistics about technological advances, violence and strife on earth—he made it look like a PowerPoint kids could have put together, without being too simple. Nira was playing her part, taking turns with Ru in narrating the slides, using the script A'ri had sent.

She started to worry when a slide with a picture of the Milky Way popped up, and Reuben said, "The mysteries of dark matter go beyond its role in a universe governed by Newtonian physics. dark matter is, in fact, a cornerstone in the way of life of an entire, alien civilization—"

Someone in the audience snorted.

A new slide, this one an old fashioned, black and white photo of miners at the mouth of a cave, so covered in coal dust that they barely looked like people. Reuben continued talking.

"—one which has learned to mine it for their own use, and in doing so, put life on Earth, and the very integrity of our solar system, at risk!"

Now there were mutterings throughout the auditorium. Billie could see a few angry faces in the crowd, people looking at each other, turning around in their chairs, whispering.

"Wait! Listen!" Nira stepped to the microphone, and a new slide showed a collection of pictures: the pyramids, fuzzy photos of UFOs, and a map of the ocean with a triangle drawn over it, among several others. "You must acknowledge that there are mysteries about our world, our own history and civilizations, that we have been unable to explain," she said, her voice vibrating with intensity. "Not to mention the question of whether life exists anywhere else in the universe!"

"We can provide you with answers to all of this," Reuben leaned in to say, as a slide with three words slid into view on the screen.

CHECK YOUR EMAIL

Among mocking jeers and sounds of impatient laughter, Billie could hear exclamations of *What? What is this? Can we go to lunch now?*

"Do it," Nira said in her bossiest voice. "Now. Get out your phones or your tablets, and check."

Billie watched as first a few, then more, and finally everyone in the room was bending over glowing screens, tapping and typing and scrolling. Nira kept talking.

"We came here today to get your attention. This email is so you can see that this is no joke. It's not a hoax or a stunt. It is life and death reality." She paused, and Billie saw people in the audience reading their screens, showing them to each other, looking up at Nira with shocked faces, then looking back at their screens again.

"You were all brought here today because yours are the finest minds, the experts who can understand what we're talking about," Reuben had taken over the mic again, his voice ringing through the auditorium. "When you have seen all the evidence, when you know that what we're saying is true, it will be up to you to convince the rest of the world, the people who can make a difference, and save not only our planet, but billions of innocent lives, lightyears away."

A final slide flicked onto the screen, and Reuben cleared his throat.

"Please, everyone, listen! As the slide says, you now have three hours. You have been sent numerous things to investigate, check and verify. Use those hours to do that—put our data through the most rigorous tests, satisfy yourselves that everything we've told you so far is fact." He paused for breath. Movement by the side of the stage caught Billie's eye. She turned her head to see her mother talking to two men in dark suits, pointing up at the window of the tech booth and then to her friends at the podium. Then she turned and started climbing the stairs onto the stage.

She hurriedly texted a message for Gaurav as Ru continued speaking.

"When those three hours have elapsed, you can all expect another email—it will explain even more, and—"

Nira saw Billie's mom approaching, and she jumped in front of Reuben. "The future survival of humankind rests on your shoulders!" she shouted into the mic, then grabbed Ru's elbow and dove behind the curtain just as Billie's mother reached the podium.

At that moment the auditorium was plunged into darkness.

People started shouting and Billie could hear movement, the sounds of confusion and fear.

"Come on, let's get out of here," Ben said, grabbing her hand and pulling her toward the rear side exit.

In the dark, Billie stumbled and banged her knee. She was letting Ben pull her along, following blindly. Behind them some of the adults were shouting for the lights to be turned on, and suddenly her mom's voice rang out over the pa system.

"Everybody stay calm. Do not try to leave until we get the lights turned on. Stay in your seats, please!"

She felt a puff of cool air hit her face, dimly made out an open door in front of her, Ben pushing it wide. They went through. The sounds of the auditorium died out when the door clicked shut.

"Come on," Ben sounded breathless, "I think this dumps us out by the cafe." He let go of her hand, and they hurried down a short hallway toward another door, outlined in daylight.

They found themselves just off the main hallway, looking across at the "Explore the Universe" exhibit entrance. To their right, museum visitors were in line for the café.

"There," Billie pointed at the sign on the wall opposite them. "There are bathrooms by the café doors. Let's change and get to the rendezvous."

Inside her stall, Billie yanked the skirt off and shoved it inside her backpack. She had some trouble unbuttoning her blouse because her hands were shaking. Finally she got it off, pulled on her t-shirt, and headed back out to find Ben.

He was waiting for her by the drinking fountain.

Trying to move quickly without drawing attention to themselves, they headed for the "How Things Fly" exhibit. Pretending to be looking at the various interactive activities, they made their way to the small video theater, a semi-darkened corner of the area that was shielded from the rest by a wall, with bench seating. Most of the people in there were younger children, some with their parents, but there were also Shae and Thomas, back in their normal school clothes, sitting at the back.

As they walked toward them, Billie's phone vibrated. She grabbed it and read the message. It was from Nira.

Found Gaurav. Too hot for us inside. Meet at Carousel.

She held the screen up for the others to see. They read it silently and nodded. After a few moments of pretending to watch the video, they moved quietly back out of the exhibit hall, down to the main entrance, and back outside into the gray afternoon.

The Carousel on the National Mall was about a block and a half away. Glancing over their shoulders now and then, they walked toward it. Nira, Reuben and Gaurav were waiting on the far side.

They huddled together, and Billie noticed for the first time how cold it was.

"Brrr," Thomas said, then grinned. "Hey," he said. "How's it going, guys?"

They all laughed, but it felt strange, slightly hysterical, and Billie shivered.

"We can't stand out here like this," Nira said, sounding serious again. "We have almost an hour before Elijah will pick us up. We need to be invisible."

"Camouflaged," Reuben corrected her, pointing across the Mall at a crowd of people. It was a group of about eighty students, all around their age, led by a guide with a red umbrella.

"Brilliant," Nira smiled at him. "Let's go catch up with our group, shall we?"

They hurried over to the group, splitting up to blend in. The guide was using a small bullhorn to give instructions for their next museum visit. "You'll have one hour to explore the Natural History Museum," she said. "Your teachers wanted me to remind you to be sure and visit the Ancient Egyptian exhibit, because there will be test questions on it!" The students around them groaned. With a toothy grin the guide waved her umbrella in the air and led them across the street and up the steps to the main entrance.

Once inside, the mass of students split off in many directions. Nira sent a text telling everyone to meet in the Human Origins area in fifteen minutes.

Following a dozen or so girls who didn't seem to notice her, Billie went upstairs to the precious gems and jewels exhibit. It was a perfect place to walk around slowly, staring at each case, though afterward Billie couldn't remember what she'd looked at; her thoughts were light years away, wondering what A'ri was doing and thinking, wishing she could contact him and tell him about everything they'd just done, how it had gone, ask what he thought about it all.

They met in the Hall of Human Origins.

"It's weird to think that we might still look like this, be living like this, if The Realm hadn't discovered our little solar system," Shae said quietly, pointing to a scene of early humans wearing furs, huddled around a small fire.

"We can't know how things would be different," Reuben pointed out, "but we probably wouldn't still be quite *that* primitive." He looked at Billie. "Well? How did it go? I mean, from the audience's perspective—do you think they...?" He let his voice trail off.

"I think they took it about the way we expected," Billie said slowly, walking over to another section of the mural. "I mean, at first they were interested, I think they liked the whole thing. But as soon as you started talking about aliens..."

"Yeah, that's when I started seeing some serious push-back," Ben nodded.

"It's all in my video," Shae said. "From the back corner, I got the entire audience *and* you guys, for the whole thing. You can see it when we get home."

Nira folded her arms and jerked her head toward the wall of humanoid skulls. They followed her, pretending to look closely at each new development in evolution. She half-whispered, "It's all up to A'ri now. His emails have to convince them."

Thomas said, "Well, we do have the videos. We can go public with everything if these guys don't do something."

Reuben was shaking his head. "That's not a good option. It's a last resort," his voice rose, and the others shushed him. "Sorry. But the chaos that going public could cause—"

"A'ri knows that," Billie reassured him. "He'll only take the public option if there's no other choice." She tried to sound calm, but the idea scared her, too.

"Hey," Ben turned to Gaurav. "What happened up in the booth? How'd you make that happen?"

"I took advantage of American stereotypes of Indian kids," Gaurav grinned. Then, with a thick Indian accent, he said, "I am the tech guru for the student group, here to conduct in the best possible way the coordination of the PowerPoint slides with my colleagues' spoken words."

"You didn't!" Nira scoffed.

"I did!" Gaurav was laughing now. "You should've seen their faces. They thought I was adorable," he waggled his head a little. "One guy tried to get me to give him the thumb drive, said he'd take care of it, but I made eyes at a lady who took my side, and he backed off. She was so busy asking me questions about 'my homeland' and what brought my family to America, she didn't pay any attention to what you guys were saying." He shrugged. "So, when I got your text about shutting it all down, it was easy to reach right under her nose and hit the blackout switch. I was out of there before they knew what happened." Ben held up a hand, and Gaurav high-fived him.

"The timing was perfect," Billie said. "What about you guys? How'd you two get off the stage without getting caught?"

"The blackout definitely helped," Nira nodded at her brother.

"Yeah," Reuben agreed. "We'd be in custody now, if we hadn't had that cover—I was sure your mom was going to get us!"

"I pulled Ru backstage. We ran for the emergency exit."

"It put us right at the end of the hallway with the café bathrooms," Reuben told them. "There was a group of little kids out there, horsing around while they waited, their teachers yelling at them—the perfect diversion. Couldn't have asked for better."

"We changed and headed for 'How Things Fly,' as planned," Nira continued. "But we saw some big guys who looked like security heading in the same direction and got scared, so we ducked into the Space Race room."

"They found me, hiding behind the V2 missile," Gaurav said. "I saw the security guards, too."

"That's when I texted you," Nira added.

"And here we are," Shae added with a sigh.

They were all quiet for a few minutes. Then Ben said, "It's almost time for Elijah to pick us up. We should head over."

They left the Natural History Museum and headed diagonally across the Mall to Jefferson avenue, where Elijah had dropped them off just a few hours earlier. An icy drizzle began to fall on them as they stood, huddled together, waiting.

"I see the car," Ben said after about five minutes. "He's a block or so down."

"Do you think your mother recognized us?" Nira suddenly asked, turning to Billie. "Do you think there's a chance—"

"I honestly don't know," Billie shook her head.

"We'll find out, one way or another, when we get home," Reuben said as the green station wagon pulled up to the curb beside them.

"Hi my little delinquent nerds!" Elijah teased as they climbed in, sliding across the back seat and buckling themselves in. "How was it?"

WATCHING AND WAITING

Billie was uneasy.

Her mom didn't come home that night, and when Billie got up Saturday morning, her father told her that she was going to be away all weekend.

"Something came up in Washington, and she has to stay up there," he explained. He didn't sound upset or worried. But then, Billie wondered, how much could Mom possibly have told him? She wouldn't give any details out over the phone, would she? *He probably just thinks it's something routine*, she thought to herself.

"Okay," she said. "Does that mean we can have pizza again?"

He laughed. "Sure, but tonight we add a salad. I don't want your mother to kill me when she comes home."

At least things with Dad seemed normal.

Sunday night was hard. She knew not to expect any messages from A'ri—he had to be extra careful now. Billie wondered if he was already communicating with some of the scientists, and maybe they were busy planning, working things out. Her need to hear from him, to be sure he was okay, didn't really rank with everything else going on.

At lunch on Monday, the crew didn't talk much while they ate. As soon as they were allowed outside for recess, they walked to the back of the field.

"Have you heard anything?" Reuben asked as soon as they were out of earshot of any other kids.

Billie shook her head. "But I didn't really expect to," she added.

"No," Nira said, hands on her hips. "Our number one job right now is just to wait and see."

"I've been watching the news a lot," Thomas said. "I keep thinking there'll be something, some sign of change..."

"Me too!" Shae said. "I even hacked into my mom's Facebook account—I added the app to my phone so I can cruise her newsfeed and see if anything shows up."

Ben laughed. "I had Elijah set me up with Instagram," he said. "It made him feel important, but it also let me see his feed." He shrugged. "Nothing important, although now I know my 'cool' big brother spends a lot of time watching cat videos," he shook his head.

"I've been checking the science publications, but I don't really expect anything to show up there this soon," Reuben said. "We should all just keep our eyes open."

"I guess we'll know by the end of the week, anyway," Gaurav said. "I mean, didn't A'ri give them a week to respond?" The others nodded.

"I don't know if it's a good sign or not," Billie said, "but my mom is still up in Washington. Dad says she'll probably be there all week."

"Now that *is* encouraging," Reuben said. "I mean, we know she was working with Dr. Menkel—if she's involved in this all week long, then they must be doing *something* up there!"

"Let's just hope it's the *right* something," Ben muttered.

The week dragged on.

Thursday night, her father had the news on while he cooked dinner. Billie was in the living room, reading, when she overheard something that caught her attention. She ran into the kitchen.

"What did that just say? Can you go back, Dad?"

He rewound the broadcast thirty seconds.

On the screen, a man was talking. Underneath him, a caption read, 'CEO of Major Social Media Organization Begins Ethics Enquiry.'

"It is my position that there is a moral responsibility that goes hand in hand with our popularity as a platform," the man was saying to a reporter. "We have crossed the line from being a business to being a guiding influence in our world, and with that comes the need to examine every aspect of what we do, and what we enable others to do."

The scene cut back to a grey-haired man behind a desk talking.

"Wow," Dad said, muting the T.V. "I never thought I'd see the day a public media corporation was willing to take an ethical stance."

"Why not?"

"Because they could lose a lot of money doing this. They've resisted anything like this up till now. I wonder why the change?"

Billie turned away from her father, her heart beating fast. She went back into the living room and picked up her book again. Only after ten minutes did she realize she was holding it upside down. Tossing it aside, she flopped onto her back and stared at the ceiling. Her brain only had room for one thought: *Could this be the beginning?*

***

On Friday, Mr. Craighton surprised her Social Studies class by handing out scripts, instead of the usual weekend home-work packets.

"I know this isn't a drama class," he said as he went around the room, "but sometimes the best way to learn something is to live through it. That's what you all are going to do!"

"Are these instructions for building a time machine?" One of the boys said. The kids around him laughed, but so did Mr. Craighton.

"Okay, Sean, very funny. The final project for our Judicial Branch Unit is going to be a mock trial. We're going to put the new environmental protection bill that's before Congress to the test!" He walked over to a poster of the Constitution and pointed to it. "We will have our own nine judges hear arguments from both sides about whether this bill is Constitu-tional, and therefore be allowed to become law." He walked to the white board and picked up a marker. "Everyone has a part to play!" he uncapped the pen and began writing the names of Supreme Court judges on the board.

"How do you put a bill on trial?" the same boy shouted out. A few others said, "Yeah," and, "I don't get it."

"Don't worry, it'll make sense as we go along." Mr. Criaghton turned around and held his arms out to the class, one of his trademark dramatic gestures. "Today we'll assign parts, and then you can start planning out your arguments and gathering evidence in teams."

Some of the kids groaned.

"If you actually *look* at your scripts, you'll see that there's a lot of room for improvisation," he smiled at the class and bounced a little on his toes. "Acting! Drama! Comedy! Guys, you can make this fun!" He turned around and wrote 'fun' on the board. Some of the kids laughed. Students mostly liked him, but he was known for being corny. "Now, how many of you watch the news?"

He looked around the room. No one raised their hands.

"Well, you're going to want to start. This new bill is all anyone's reporting on, due to the unprecedented speed it was developed and the total bipartisan support it's receiving. But don't get any funny ideas," he wagged his finger at the class. "Just because Congress is in agreement for once, doesn't mean we're not having our mock trial."

The class giggled, some kids rolled their eyes, and Mr. Craighton began assigning parts.

Billie had stopped paying attention.

Unprecedented speed and bipartisan agreement on an environmental protection bill?!

Where had that come from? Since when did both sides agree on protecting the environment, and passing a law about it? The country, and therefore Congress, was totally divided on the subject, red versus blue...

Until now.

It had to be another sign of progress. A'ri said that conflict and problems were caused by the Gen on purpose, to make dark matter easier for them to take, and the way to shut them down was to stop the problems in the world.

This could be a step in that direction. Along with the social media thing the other night.

If only I could talk to A'ri and ask him!

Her phone buzzed, and she looked down at the screen. It was the group chat.

Ru: Can we get together?

Ben: Sure

Gaurav: When?

Shae: After school?

Nira: We can't—but tomorrow? Our house?

On the bus ride home from school, Billie heard a couple of kids who were also in her social studies class talking. One of them, a girl who'd been assigned a role on the prosecution's side, thought the new law was a good thing.

"Wouldn't it be nice if everyone could agree on things like taking care of the environment and stopping global warming because the experts told us it's a problem, instead of just take a side because they were 'red' or 'blue'?" she said.

The boy was more cynical, saying he didn't think it would last, it must be a stunt of some kind. "Just follow the money...my dad says no one does anything in Washington if there isn't a payout attached," he said smugly.

The payout is for the whole world, Billie thought. *But how can a world accustomed to fighting so much be made to see that?*

***

They were all at Nira and Gaurav's house by 11:00 the next morning. Reuben was jubilant, going around giving each of them high fives and cheering, "We did it! It worked, guys, it worked!"

"You think the thing in Congress is a sign?" Billie asked timidly.

"Of course it is!" Reuben crowed. "And what about the social media guy? Did you see that?"

"I missed that, what was it?" Shae asked.

Gaurav explained it to her. "But that's only two things, Ru. I'm not sure we can say definitively—"

"No, no, I know," Reuben flopped into a beanbag chair. He was still beaming. "But it's a good start—and revolutionary! I mean, unprecedented! *It's begun!*"

Nira tried to bring him back down to earth.

"But this is *only* the beginning," she said. "These are good signs, yes, but A'ri's plan has to happen globally. It's all or nothing, really."

"Have you heard from him?" Shae asked Billie.

"Still no word," Billie sighed.

"What about other countries?" Thomas asked. "We may be a world power, but like Nira said, the changes have to be global."

They all looked blankly at each other. Even Reuben stopped smiling and shook his head.

"I was so excited, I didn't think to look for news from other countries," he admitted.

"We'll just have to keep our eyes open," Shae said.

"Is your mom back yet?" Ben asked.

"No, but she called last night and said she'll probably be home tomorrow," Billie said. "Dad says she's working on a new project. She's going to have to be up in D.C. a lot for a while."

"That seems hopeful," Reuben perked up a little.

"Are you going to tell her?" Gaurav asked. "I mean about A'ri, and us, and you?"

Billie blew out a lungful of air and shrugged. "I don't know," she said. "I keep thinking about it, wondering if I should…"

"There's no hurry," Shae said gently. "I bet, if the right moment comes when you should tell her, you'll know it."

They sat around talking for almost two hours, reliving the day in D.C. and everything that had happened since, getting no homework done. Finally, Nira stood up.

"I'm sorry guys, but we have piano in half an hour," she said. "We've got to get ready to go."

One by one they said goodbye as their parents came to pick them up. Billie was the last to go.

"See you Monday," Nira called out, waving from the front porch.

"Let us know if you hear anything," Gaurav shouted over his sister's shoulder. She turned around, shoving him into the house ahead of her.

Billie laughed as she buckled her seatbelt.

***

Sunday night Billie went to bed at the normal time. Dad came to tuck her in.

"Good night," she said, hugging him. "Tell Mom to come in when she gets home, no matter how late it is, okay?"

"You bet, Billie-bean," Dad said, hugging her back.

She rolled onto her side and stared out her window, waiting for sleep to come. Just as her eyelids were starting to feel heavy, there was a buzzing on her nightstand and her phone lit up. Sitting up in bed, she grabbed the phone and checked the screen.

It was A'ri.

Hi!

I'm so glad it's you! How are you? Is everything okay there? Are you safe?

Everything's good. Sorry I haven't been in touch. It's been...busy.

What's happening? Can you tell me?

Not too much right now, but I'll tell you everything later, when I have more time. Most important: the scientists are on board, and we're get-

ting lots of cooper-
ation—you guys were
perfect!

That's amazing!

Have you seen things
happening?

Yes—a little.

First steps only. More
to come. I have to go—
things here still dan-
gerous... But first: you
should know that one
Earther has been a
real leader in getting
people there to work
together.

????

Your mother. And...I
told her about you.
I thought she should
know about...every-
thing.

Wow.

Don't worry! She was
great about the whole
thing!

Thanks for telling me.

> **No, thank YOU, Billie.**
> **Gotta go.**

OK—be careful!

Billie fell asleep cradling her phone. It was still folded into her right hand when her mother quietly pushed open the bedroom door and sat beside her on the bed.

"Billie? Honey, I'm home," she said softly.

Billie stirred. Her eyelids fluttered, then snapped open. "Mom!" she sat up and wrapped her arms around her neck, knocking the phone onto the floor. "You're home!"

"Mmmm," Her mom hugged her back, then pulled away. Looking down at the floor where the phone landed, she raised her eyebrows. "It seems like maybe getting you that phone was a lot bigger deal than we realized, eh?" Billie reached down to get her phone and looked up as her dad came in.

"Hey," he said, "isn't there someone who's supposed to be asleep in here?"

Billie's mom looked back at her. "I have a feeling that this young lady isn't going to get back to sleep for a while," she looked up at her husband's puzzled face. "Billie and I need to fill you in on a few things," she paused, turning back to her daughter, "and I have a lot of questions that need answers, too."

Billie searched her mother's eyes, trying to see if she was angry. "You've talked to A'ri already, right?" she asked.

"Yes, I have."

"He told me," Billie glanced down at her phone, biting her lip. "He said you were okay with everything."

Her mother nodded. "I think that's accurate," she said. "But that doesn't mean I don't still have a lot of blanks I'd like you to fill in for me."

"Who's A'ri? What are you two talking about?" Her father stood framed in the doorway, hands on his hips, a small frown on his face.

"Come on," Mom stood up and held out her hand to Billie. "Let's go downstairs and bring your father into the picture." Billie took her hand and climbed out of bed. "Don't worry, everything's all right." She put her hand on her husband's arm and squeezed. "But fair warning: you're not going to believe what we have to tell you."

CHAPTER

29

A'RI

He walked down the hall at a brisk pace—shuffling was a thing of the past now. He realized his face was showing preoccupation, worry—and he smiled. *No more pleasant neutrality.*

He rounded a corner and went through the doors into the cantina, pausing to search the room. At the far end, near the nourishment dispensary, stood Sh'nok, the Supervisor he was looking for.

Shaking his head and enjoying the feeling of his smile widening again, he corrected himself. – *'Gen Liaison,' not 'Supervisor'. Not anymore.*

He walked up to it. "Liaison Sh'nok, Central Coordination has reordered your placement. You are needed at the MC." Looking directly into the former Supervisor's eyes, A'ri nodded respectfully but did not divert his gaze. At first Sh'nok looked surprised. Then he saw its mouth grow tense, its fingers clench, sure signs of anger. Once, this would have meant certain physical punishment, a bad beating, but now A'ri continued to hold its gaze, and after a moment it relaxed again, nodding back.

"Very well," it sniffed. Another Liaison approached. A'ri recognized it as the one who had beaten C'un so badly just over a year ago. The cantina grew quiet as everyone nearby watched.

"Is this Blank troubling you, officer?"

"No," Sh'nok looked uncertain. "Just accepting new orders, sir. It's delivering the message."

A'ri took a deep breath, looking each of them in the eyes as he spoke. "With respect sirs, I wear the Purple Badge," he said, pointing to his left shoulder where it was on display. "I am he/him. Please use my correct terminology."

Silence. The diners seemed to be holding their breath, waiting to see how their former Supervisors would respond. Though negotiations had shifted things dramatically over the past year, this was still new for all of them. There had been incidents...

"Put your eyes where they belong, Blank," growled the second Liaison. "You need to remember who you're speaking to," it took a step toward A'ri, raising its fist at the same time.

From the nearest table, there was movement. A'ri looked over his shoulder and saw one of his barracks mates standing.

"Yellow Badge: she/her, Sir," she said.

At another table, someone else stood up. "Purple Badge: he/him, Sir," he called out.

Around the room the others stood, claiming their genders. A'ri looked at the Liaison, and saw disgust on its face—was fear there, too?

"Come on, P'urnt," Sh'nok said, reaching over to push its arm down and stepping between it and A'ri. "Let's go." They left the cantina together.

A'ri gazed around the room. At least a third of all the Blanks —no, *the Oh'hani*—were standing, proudly wearing badges to indicate their engendering. Some were further along in the process than others. There were those whose gender he could tell without needing to look at their badge, but everyone went at their own pace, and the badges kept things simple. Most of those who were still sitting wore the orange badge, indicating gender neutrality and a preference for it/they/them, but even some of them had stood.

Best of all, on their faces he saw *feelings*: excitement, fear, confidence, joy—all the things they'd been hiding inside for so long, at last allowed and acceptable.

He smiled, feeling his own joy bubble up inside, and left the cantina.

He was due at Central Coordination soon.

Thinking about the meeting to come, and what his role would be, he almost didn't notice the door on his left as he walked by. He paused, putting his hand against it, remembering the last time he'd used the storage room, the final transmission he'd sent.

It was only a few cycles after his last communication with Billie. Things on earth happened quickly—the interference filters he'd sent them had worked well. Once they could see the Realm's influence on their world, they acted fast, taking steps to shut out the transmissions and disable the various manipulation operations. As he'd known it would, this drastically slowed down the dark matter mining, cutting the Realm's energy production. Within only three cycles, his own natalsphere started experiencing power reductions, and more and more Blanks were being furloughed, confined to barracks, their nourishment rations cut. In his secret monitoring of the censored information channels, A'ri was reading stories about desperate shortages and massive setbacks in the Military's ability to prepare for the coming war.

He knew the time had come for his final move.

A'ri visited his hidden Surface one last time, using it to send everything he had, every file, every piece of information, all his engineered ways to move secretly through the Realm's transmissions, and records of everything he'd done with the Earthers. It was such a massive data package, he knew this one, last transmission would give him away. But he had to get it to M'ira, to let the Oh'hani homeworlders know that now was their moment. The Realm was weak and uncertain; they had to move immediately to begin the revolution.

With a swipe of his stylus, it was done. He calculated that he had mere moments to clear the space, erasing any evidence of his having been there.

He was right.

Halfway down the hall, on his way to barracks, the alarm sounded. The urgent, marching steps of six Enforcers echoed behind him—his final signal had been traced to the storage room. He'd cleared out just in time.

Three agonizing days passed. A'ri was unable to sleep, waiting for a sign of something happening. When it came, it wasn't at all what he'd expected.

On the fourth day, public broadcasts were reporting that the Realm had extended an offer to meet with O'hani leaders, hear their demands, and begin negotiations for peaceful coexistence.

The Realm made the first move? And toward *peace*?!

A'ri was stunned.

During his shiftwork later that day, he noticed the familiar stutter on his work surface. When he was certain the Supervisor couldn't see, he opened his secret communication files and found a message waiting for him.

> Received files. Very use-
> ful. Gen negotiations a
> red herring. Trust no one.
> Await my next.
>
> -M'ira

A'ri quickly closed the link and got back to work. As he mechanically completed the rest of his shift, his brain worked furiously, trying to understand what it all meant. But without more information, he could only guess and hope that soon he'd find out more.

He didn't have long to wait.

Once the Realm made their offer public, things moved fast. It was agreed by both sides that their interactions be facilitated by a third party—a tech-oriented natalsphere, highly regarded among the Gen to appease their side, but with a trained, highly skilled Blank at the helm, representing the O'hani.

A'ri was summoned by a Supervisor from his morning meal the next day. Escorted to Central Coordination by three Enforcers, he was told by the HeadGen itself of his new role as Communication Facilitator in the negotiations between The Realm and the O'hani.

"Don't let it go to your head, Blank," The HeadGen snarled dismissively. "The Realm isn't going to humor your kind for long," and it chuckled darkly, dismissing him with a wave.

There was a lot for A'ri to do. It was a big responsibility, but now he could work at his own pace, not having to hide the speed and sophistication of his thinking. He was allowed to select the best and brightest of his natalsphere to help him, too. It was an exciting new challenge, and even more, he was making friends.

Nothing happened quickly, but a few agreements were put in place to avoid problems while the leaders worked things out: new rights and privileges for Blanks throughout the system, as well as limitations for the Gen. It wasn't perfect. There were violent incidents in some of the natalspheres.

M'ira rarely communicated privately with A'ri, but her messages to him continued to warn him not to trust the Gen, nor the very negotiations they were engaged in. Reading between the lines, he suspected that she feared the Realm was far from ready to give in peacefully. For now, without the resources they needed for forceful domination, they weren't fighting back...but he had a feeling that peace wouldn't last forever.

In the meantime, today's Negotiation Summit was addressing how to ease the way for both sides into the New Order, as some were calling it.

But before the meeting began, he had something else to take care of. With no need to transmit using secret backchannels, A'ri entered the Coms Hub in the Central Coordination office and opened a transmission line. He checked some instruments—it should be just after 9:00 pm on Sunday, Earth Time.

Billie?

A'ri! I've missed you so much!

I've missed you, too. How are you?

Great! Things are still changing here...but you probably know that!

I've been keeping an eye on things, LOL!

What about you?

We've got a long way to go, but there's progress. I have so much to tell you!

EPILOGUE: ONE YEAR LATER

Scientist Confirms Discovery

Stanford Astrophysicist publishes findings to revolutionize energy production

Stanford, CA. *Dr. Richard Menkel, world-renowned astrophysicist, published his latest findings in the journal* **Science** *last week, which have been hailed as revolutionary by scientists and world leaders alike.*

Menkel's work on dark matter, an esoteric and poorly understood mystery material in the Universe, has proven it can be a game-changing source of energy.

"It's not merely a new source of energy," Dr. James Standish of Harvard University explains. "It is a substance which is completely renewable, creates no pollution, and can almost immediately be converted for use in every area of daily life."

There are practical considerations that must be accounted for, of course. Dr. Menkel is convening a research team whose sole purpose will be to create the mechanisms necessary to tap into our solar system's supply of dark matter and convert it for use.

"This process will take time," he wrote in a statement released to the press last week. "We may be looking at a decade of trial and error before we can implement the use of dark matter to fuel our world."

In the statement, he goes on to predict that by the end of the century, the entire planet could be fueled by this mysterious substance, making fossil fuels and their negative environmental side effects an artifact of the past.

The hand that placed the article on the gleaming wood of the conference table had a slight tremor. Its owner squinted around at the five others who'd listened as he read, reading their expressions.

"Gentlemen," he spoke, his gravelly voice slicing into the silence. "This will not do."

A handsome man in long robes with a beard streaked with white leaned forward, placing his hands on the table. "We cannot allow this."

The only one not sitting was a tall, dark-haired woman. She stood away from the others in a corner of the room, staring out of the floor-to-ceiling windows that overlooked forested hills. "We must embrace it, of course," her words seemed to curl as she spoke to them, sharp-edged and accented. "The world must see us unified in our enthusiasm." She turned away from

Elisabeth Wathen is a teacher, writer, poet, and musician. She lives with her husband and a loving orange tabby cat in their historic farmhouse, teaching and writing surrounded by the beauty of the Catskills in Upstate New York.